BEST GAY
BONDAGE EROTICA

BEST GAY
BONDAGE EROTICA

Edited by
Richard Labonté

CLEIS
PRESS

Cover design: Scott Idleman
Cover photograph: Jackson Photografix
Text design: Frank Wiedemann
Cleis logo art: Juana Alicia
First Edition.
10 9 8 7 6 5 4 3 2 1

For Asa,
Bound by love

Contents

INTRODUCTION: BLAME IT ON VICTOR MATURE

Can it be as simple as this: we desire now what we desired then?

Then, I wanted a lanky, redheaded lad with supple limbs and a large graceful nose. I had that tall boy—with freckles!—for almost a year, before we were even legal, until his family's move to a new military base took him out of my life. Now, I have loved many other men: some tall, some short, some slim, some stout, some fair-haired, some dark-haired, some fair-skinned, some dark-skinned, some with just a hint of red about their heads, even some with no hair at all, several decades beyond my redheaded first love.

But the imprinting remains. My head turns at the sight of a slender man, a tall man with supple limbs, a noble nose, and red hair. My head sometimes turns at two out of three. In truth, my head will turn simply at the sight of a redhead.

I remain now what I was then, am excited now by what excited me then.

Without getting all theoretical and psychological here, I'm

pretty sure it's the same with amorphous desire as it is with the memory of a real person. That's why some younger men yearn for older, why some men lust after muscle, why some men find heft and hair erotic, why some men thrill to the sight of a firefighter or a police officer—or a UPS delivery man—in uniform, and why some men are stimulated by wrestling, or spanking, or piss, or shit. Or silk. It's what turned them on, early on. Why that should be so, in the first place, I'll leave to the theorists, and the shrinks.

For some men, it's all about the ties that bind. Naughty knots. The struggle against restraints. The rush of abandoning control. Sometimes even the absence of senses. How does it start? A ten-year-old sitting in front of the black-and-white TV in years past sees Chuck Connors in "The Rifleman" or Clint Eastwood in "Rawhide" muscling against Western rope, and a desire is born. (Is it a kinkier desire if the turn-on originated from watching Davy Jones, Micky Dolenz, Mike Nesmith, and Peter Tork—in psychedelic color!—in "The Monkees" episode "Your Friendly Neighborhood Kidnappers"?) Even now, in an era where bondage of all sorts streams across laptop screens, images of The Rock and Seann William Scott bound together in *The Rundown* (2003) can turn on today's questioning and soon-queer teen, and titillate older homos with an eye for the bound guy. And bondage fans of a certain age will forever have Victor Mature in *Samson and Delilah*....

And they'll have the stories in this collection: the metal cuffs, latex suits, silk ties, strong tape, loops of rope and leather, a classic harness—the tools of a particular erotic trade—and the men who top and the men who bottom for the pleasure of our imaginations. Then, and now.

Richard Labonté
Bowen Island, British Columbia

KIDNAPPING CHRIS

Jeff Mann

He's been out for a while. Rob's checked on him twice. A train's rocked and roared past the house, but Chris has slept on, sagging and snoring in the dark.

Outside, it's late summer. Queen Anne's lace edges the pastures with floating discs of snow, and Joe-Pye weed lines the ditches along the dirt road, its tall flowers like shaggy wigs the hue of old rose. Rob and Mark's little farm needs water badly; rain's been sparse this summer in southwest Virginia. The tomato plants, hot peppers, and zinnias are all half-wilted. After Rob slips the pie in the oven, he fills a can with tap water, steps outside, and gently pours it over the limp-leaved plants. He'd like to sit on the porch and watch silver maple boughs sway in the warm breeze—every breeze in August is a blessing—but he might not hear Chris out here. Chris should be coming to in an hour or two and he's responsible for Chris now, entirely responsible. So Rob steps back inside, mixes a mint julep, hurriedly does up the dishes, then hits the couch with a new fantasy novel.

If Chris wakes up in time for dinner, Rob will fry them up corn cut off the cob, browned in bacon grease, spiced up with cayenne. He's got homemade biscuits in the freezer, so he could heat them up, top them with country ham, mayonnaise, sliced tomatoes picked fresh from the garden. Then there's the pie, coconut cream, due out of the oven soon, Chris's favorite kind, as Rob well knows. Rob likes cooking for handsome men. He likes taking care of them. One thing's for sure: Chris isn't likely to lose weight during his sojourn here.

Rob's halfway through his drink and beginning another chapter of the novel when Chris regains consciousness in the basement, directly below the sofa where Rob comfortably sprawls. Like bubbles released when the bottom of a pond's disturbed by a dropped anchor, Chris floats up out of darkness and silence. What he finds is not light spangling the surface, however, but more darkness and silence, a chrysalis entirely enveloping him. What he sees and hears is nothingness. What he feels is constriction and discomfort.

Where? he thinks, shifting in the chair, lifting his head and shaking it. There's no sound but blood pumping in his ears, and, beyond the cinder block walls, the chirring of insects in summer meadows. There's no light at all. Rob's careful creation of this space has seen to that. There isn't even a crack of light under the door.

Chris shakes his head again. His temples are throbbing and wet. Drops of sweat tickle his cheeks in their descent. His mouth is dry, his jaws are sore. His limbs ache. He groans. Where the fuck is he? Why does he feel so bad? Why is it so dark, so quiet?

Removing his hat would help. As usual, Chris is wearing a cowboy hat; he can feel its weight on his head, its sweatband on his brow. He wants to take it off, to wipe the moisture off his temples, to massage his aching head. He tries to do all those things. He fails. He cannot move his arms.

It takes a few frantic seconds of tugging and thrashing for Chris to understand his situation. Now he's scared. His heart races; the blood rushes through him, making his head hurt worse. His throat, belly, and scrotum are tight with fear.

What his struggle reveals is this: he's bound to a chair, like some hapless character in a Western. He's shirtless—he can gauge this by the cool air on his torso, shoulders, and arms—though otherwise he's still clothed, he knows, for, as devoid of light as his new world is, he can feel the presence of his hat, belt, jeans, and cowboy boots. His hands are secured together behind the chair; something rough, dense, and narrow is wrapped tightly around his crossed wrists, chafing the skin as he struggles. Rope, Chris correctly assumes. More rope is knotted around his arms and elbows, securing them to the chair back. More rope, criss-crossing his bare chest above and below his nipples, makes it impossible for Chris to move his torso more than an inch or two in any direction. Another round of rope cuts into the furry curve of his belly, increasing his immobility. His thighs are spread and bound to the chair's seat; his booted ankles are tied to the chair's back legs at such a height that only his toes touch the basement floor.

Upstairs, in early evening's copper light, Rob's finished his drink; downstairs, in the unmitigated blackness, Chris has begun to panic. He's a big tough redneck from Texas, he's had his share of bar brawls and ass-whippings both given and received. But he's never been this disoriented or powerless. He rocks and squirms, trying to work his wrists and ankles loose, twisting and straining his chest against the rough rope till he's breathing hard and hurting. Fright and exertion make him pant and curse, but that only leads to another unwelcome discovery: it's hard to breathe through his mouth, and his swear words come out muffled. When he bites down in frustration, his teeth sink into a balled-up rag his captor has stuffed in his mouth, entirely filling it. This is the reason his tongue is dry and his jaws ache. When Chris tries to work the rag out with his tongue, he can feel tape tightening over his lips, tugging at his cheeks and the back of his neck. Not only can he barely move, he can barely speak.

Fuck! Goddamn it! Chris would like to shout for help, but that's what stupid women do in distress, and besides, he figures any noise he makes will simply summon his captor, whatever bastard has bound and gagged him and left him here. *Who the hell has done this?* he wonders, suddenly as enraged as he is frightened, searching his memory and coming up with nothing. He can't remember the events of today. He tries to shake amnesia from his head, as if it were a cloud of cigar smoke like those he regularly emits in honky-tonks, something to be dismissed with the wave of a hand. This cloud will not disperse.

Upstairs, Rob rises to mix another drink. In the cellar, Chris hears the creak of floorboards overhead. Now he knows for sure he's not alone, his captor is near. In a careful silence broken only by snorts of fear and rage, by low, rag-stifled cursing, Chris works to free himself. He stops occasionally to rest, to catch his breath, before beginning the fight again. He tosses his head like a wild horse, till his cowboy hat, dislodged at last, skips across the floor. The rag packed in his mouth grows wet with the furious gnashing of his teeth. The rope cuts into his flesh; the skin of his wrists grows raw; the muscles of his bare chest and arms chafe and bruise. He will get loose, he will get out of here, by god, he will get loose.

Rocking from side to side, Chris feels the taut ropes over his upper chest give a little. This gives him hope. He rocks harder. He rocks harder. He rocks too hard. He sways, he tips over. His bare shoulder slams into the concrete floor, pain jolts through him with a gasp.

Chris is sobbing softly now. He's alone, there's no one to see him cry, so he can afford to break down. His bare sides shake. His head lolls against the gritty floor. A few tears escape. His shoulder throbs and stings, bleeding a little. His hands clench and unclench, straining still in their tight circles of rope, continuing their futile fight for freedom, but listlessly now, because he's in pain and he's exhausted. He breathes hard through his nose and fights back the tears, willing himself to calm down, to shake off this welling terror, to be a man, not a sissy, to figure out what to do, what the fuck to do.

Chris lies there, aching on the floor, for half an hour before his struggles taper off entirely and he finally calls for help. He's tentative at first, utterly humiliated by such a necessity, then, when no one responds, he increases the volume. Despite the thick gag, a big man like him can make some noise, though the actual words—"Help me! For fuck's sake, help!"—are entirely unintelligible. Finally, Chris lifts his head from the floor, sucks in cool cellar air through his nose, fills his lungs, and simply roars.

Upstairs there's a thump—Rob's dropped his novel—then heavy footsteps, doors slamming, someone thunking down the cellar stairs. Click of a lock, and the door opens.

Dim light falls over Chris. Footsteps across the floor. Bare hairy feet by his cheek. Chris looks up as best he can at the broad silhouette of his abductor. "*Help* me, you fucker!" Chris grunts. *Mmmm mmm mm mmm!* is what Rob hears.

"Hey, handsome, you're awake already! What are you doing on the floor? Did you hurt yourself?" Chris is a big man—used to play college football—but Rob is even bigger. With no effort at all, he's wrapped an arm around Chris's waist, grabbed the back of the chair with his other hand, and righted Chris as if he weighed no more than an adolescent girl.

"Ah, you're bleeding," says Rob, touching Chris's blood-smudged shoulder. "We'll have to wrap that up."

Chris looks up at his captor, gathering breath to shout with fury. Instead he gasps and stares. Not only is the voice familiar, but the bearded face, round glasses, hairy chest, and beer belly revealed in the gray light of the open door are all familiar too.

"Yes, Chris, it's me," Rob says, grinning down at him. "I guess you don't remember this afternoon very well, eh?" He smoothes Chris's mussed hair, strokes his brown sideburns, then bends down and kisses first his wet brow and then his taped-tight mouth. "Why are you making such a fuss? You used to claim abduction scenarios were a fantasy of yours. Haven't you always wanted this?"

*Ummm mmm! Ummmm **mmmm!*** Chris shakes his head violently. Abduction might be a hot fantasy, but reality's another matter. He never asked for any of this. Tugging at his bonds again, he glares at Rob, *mmmffff*s some more. *Let me loose, asshole!* is what he's trying to say. *Why the hell are you doing this? Let me loose!*

All garbled, but Rob can figure out from the look in Chris's face—shimmering meld of fear, anger, and confusion—what he's asking. "Nope, sorry, I'm not untying you yet. This is all for your own good." Chris snorts in response, rolling his eyes with outrage.

"Check it out: we finished all this last week, just for you," Rob says, lighting a few candles around the room. Wick by flickering wick, the space comes clear: a large, windowless room, walls painted black, a stereo system, a sling hanging from the ceiling, a St. Andrew's cross against the wall, a padded paddle-bench, a shelf displaying various implements, sex toys Chris remembers from another life, one he recanted a good while back.

Rob pushes a button. The stereo lights up. Gregorian chants fill the room. The music's meant to be relaxing, but, in response, Chris strains his torso against the rope till it indents his fleshy pecs and belly; he twists his wrists till they burn; he rocks and growls.

"Chris, baby, *stop* it. You'll hurt yourself. You're not getting loose. You know I know how to rope a man...plus, just in case, well, now that you're awake and seem determined to resist..." Rob reaches for something in the candlelight, then holds it up in front of Chris. "Remember this? Your favorite, right?"

Duct tape. Candlelight shimmers off the shiny silver-gray. Chris groans, shaking his head. Pulling loose a long section of it, Rob wraps it around Chris's chest, reinforcing the rope. "Guys can squirm out of rope sometimes, but there's no way a man can escape tape. Isn't that why you love it?" Rob chuckles, circling Chris, tightly applying the tape to his arms and torso, careful to leave his nipples exposed, finally cutting it with scissors and smoothing the end against the Celtic cross tattooed on Chris's left biceps. "When this stuff comes off later, you're going to wish your chest weren't so hairy," Rob says, ruffling the dark fur on Chris's pecs. "You might regret that handsome goatee too."

When Rob starts wrapping up Chris's wrists, that's when Chris loses all control. Dignity be damned. He thrashes crazily, frantically; he screams into his gag, his customary baritone gone shrill with hysteria. Immediately Rob drops the roll of tape. He seizes Chris's face in his hands, holding him still. "Hey! *Hey*!" Rob slaps his cheek lightly, so lightly it might be a love-tap, a caress. Chris stops his struggle, staring up at Rob, his wide brown eyes meeting Rob's light blue ones.

"Chris, for god's sake, no one's going to hurt you, okay?"

says Rob, stroking his goateed chin. "We're going to take care of you, all right? You know us, Mark and me. We love you, Chris. We got you, Chris. We're doing this for you. Just think of it as an intervention."

Chris hangs loosely in his bonds now, all fight gone. "You gonna behave," Rob says, more of an order than a question. Chris nods.

Taking advantage of his prisoner's sudden submission, Rob finishes the tape-work: wrists, then ankles, then thighs. With each ripping sound of the tape, with each tight application around his limbs, with each snip of the scissors, Chris grows weaker, more pliant in his powerlessness. Now that he knows it's Rob who's holding him, he knows he's safe. Rob would never harm him. The dwindling of fear allows other feelings to surface. By the time Rob's finished taping him up, Chris's cock, to his embarrassment and amazement, is hard in his jeans. He prays that Rob won't notice in such dim light. His reluctant tumescence tells him that Rob's right, though Chris hates to admit it: when they were together, Chris loved rough roped-up scenes like this.

"You want some water?"

Chris nods. *Please* is the soft word rag and tape hinder.

"All right, lover. I'm going to take that tape off your mouth now. You can shout as much as you want, 'cause we're way out in the country, and we're underground. No one's going to hear you, so you might as well save your voice for civilized conversation, okay?"

Chris nods. He's so worn out from struggle and shock he can hardly lift his head. Rob fetches the scissors from the floor, then reaching behind his captive's left ear very carefully cuts the tape and then very slowly unpeels it. It hurts Chris, pulling on his hair and goatee. He squints and winces. "Sorry, baby," Rob soothes.

Finally the tape is off. Rob eases the soaked rag out of Chris's mouth. "Thanks," Chris groans, stretching the stiffness from his jaw. He's such a well-bred country boy that he's mannerly even in extremity. Rob massages Chris's face, the firm and tender touch Chris has always savored. "I'm sorry we had to do this to you," Rob whispers. "But you need this. We all know you do. You're going to be all right. We're going to keep you till you know who you are."

Then Rob kisses him. Chris resists for a minute—Rob has abducted him, he's holding him against his will, Chris should bite his fucking tongue off—but then he gives in, opening his dry mouth to Rob's moist probing. After all, this is a man he has kissed before. This is a man whose body he's worshipped, who has worshipped his body. In that other life, before Chris found God and married Tammy.

Rob tastes of bourbon. Chris would kill for a shot of bourbon.

There's a skittering at the door, a clicking of claws. A shaggy black dog pushes her way into the room. Rob laughs, pulling back from the kiss. He pats the dog's flank, saying, "Chris, you remember Missy. She's going to help us take care of you."

Chris licks his lips, smiling weakly. He settles back into his bonds. Part of him likes the tightness around his wrists and ankles; it reminds him of many a hot time with Rob, when they lived together in Craig County. Missy circles excitedly about, then, at Rob's command, collapses into a dog bed beneath the suspended sling. Rob fetches a pitcher and glass from somewhere behind Chris, pours water, lifts the glass to Chris's lips. Chris gulps and gulps till the glass is empty.

"Thanks," Chris murmurs. He leans back against the chair and sighs. He looks up at Rob and furrows his brow. "So what the hell?" Chris is trying to be calm now, despite the miasma of anxiety, confusion, and arousal bubbling in his brain.

Rob sighs back. He feels Chris's bound hands—still warm, circulation seems fine. He pulls a chair out of the corner, a chair identical to the one Chris is bound to. Rob's pushing three hundred pounds of muscle and belly; the chair creaks loudly as he sits back heavily and crosses his arms. He's barefoot, bare-chested, clad only in raggedy denim shorts. He's even hairier than Chris, with a thick black pelt covering his chest and his solid, round belly. His arms are bigger than Chris remembers. He looks like a brute, a biker, a criminal, black hair falling over his brow, except for the wire-rimmed glasses and the kindness in his eyes. In the old days, Chris was his boy. When they were lovers, Chris called him Daddy.

"God, you look so fine…" Rob's glance takes in Chris's half-naked body. "We're going to make you feel so good." He shakes his head, pushing back sweet visions of their future to come, and starts over again.

"So, how and why, right?"

Chris nods. He looks so whipped, so broken, slumping sweatily in his bonds. He breaks Rob's heart.

"Don't you want me to bandage up that shoulder?" Rob touches the wound. Chris winces, shrugging off solicitude.

"No," says Chris. "Not now. Now, I want to know…" He drops his gaze to the tape creasing his chest and belly, then looks at Rob with a kind of quizzical desperation.

And so Rob explains: what led them here and what Chris can't remember. He starts with their five years together, years rich with rough sex but fraught with Chris's Baptist guilt. He speaks of that Christian tract Chris brought home from the Roanoke Airport. He speaks of Chris's consequent conversion, his abandonment of Rob, his fervent churchgoing, his devotion to Exodus International's ex-gay movement, his three-year-long marriage to Tammy. He reminds Chris of those surreptitious visits he made to Rob and Mark, Rob's new lover, three-ways Chris craved but could handle only when he was staggering-drunk. He reminds Chris of those many mornings the three of them woke together, snuggled side by side in Rob and Mark's big bed, how hungover and sick with shame Chris would always be, full of regret, always quick to flee back to his wife, swearing he'd never fall into sin again.

Most recently, Rob points out, there's been Chris's constant drinking, his divorce, his long unemployment after being fired from the Radford munitions plant; his self-hatred, isolation, and despair; his sudden avoidance of Rob and Mark. And, a month ago, the DUI, when Chris drove into a ditch, banged himself up pretty badly, lost his license. That was the turning point, Rob admits. When he saw Chris in the hospital, his bruised face half-sunk in the pillow, that's when he decided to intervene.

Now Rob describes the afternoon chemistry won't let Chris remember. After months of phone-slurred reasons not to visit them, lunch today with Rob and Mark, the Texas Roadhouse in Christiansburg, a neutral place, a straight place, where Chris knew his damned desire wouldn't get out of hand. The date-rape drug Rob had heard about from college students he counseled. Chris's several Bud Lights, one of them unusually bitter, his drunkenness and confusion, a burly Texan weaving through the parking lot, supported by two big buddies. The back of Mark's van, Chris's weak struggles, his loss of consciousness, Rob's swift skill with rope and tape. The drive down Vicker's Switch, careful lugging of a bound man down cellar stairs, several hours of snoring in the dark.

Back to this here and now, Rob finishing his story thus: "You were my boy once, Chris. Now you are again. You were killing yourself, but we're going to save you. You're a gay man, lover, you're a bottom. These are things to be proud of, not to hate, not to cut out of your heart. We love you, and we're going to keep you here till you love yourself."

Chris is stunned. What can he say? He's silent as Rob fetches hydrogen peroxide and bandages his shoulder. He's silent in the dungeon's dimness, listening to music while Rob cooks upstairs. He's silent save for an occasional "Thanks" or "That's really good" as Rob feeds him fried corn, biscuits with country ham and tomatoes, coconut cream pie. Rob has chosen this menu, Chris knows, because these are some of his favorite foods, ones Rob used to prepare for him years ago. It's clear that Rob intends to give Chris everything that pleases him, short of the freedom and the bourbon he keeps asking for.

"Did you enjoy that?" Rob asks, wiping meringue from Chris's fur-framed lips.

"Yeah, a lot. You were always real good to me before I..." Chris trails off.

"No regrets, handsome. This is a new day. This is a new marriage. Mark and you and me." Rob piles the dirty dishes on a tray, then looks at his watch.

"I've got to fetch Mark from work pretty soon. His bike is in the shop. So I have to leave you here for about an hour. Think you'll be all right?"

"Yeah, I guess," says Chris.

Picking the roll of tape off the toy-table, Rob tugs off a long strip.

"Ah, naw, man!" Chris pleads. "You said no one could hear!"

"Don't try to fool me, lover. Now you know you're safe, you're turned on. I saw that hard-on in your pants. I want you gagged, you want gagged. Right?"

Chris blushes, staring down at the denim-covered bulge of

betrayal between his thighs. He shakes his head sheepishly.

Rob chortles. "Bull*shit*! Tell me what you want. Ball-gag, bit-gag, plug-gag? I've got all your favorites. What's your pleasure?"

Chris looks toward the table's array of implements. He flushes further. He shakes his head again, stammering, "Y-you know, someone's gonna be l-looking for me.... What about Tammy? And—"

"We told her you were joining the Peace Corps, and, besides, she's written you off as a drunk. You don't have any family left. You stopped attending church months ago, when you started boozing so hard. We've paid your rent for the next six months. No one will be looking for you. *We're* your family, hot stuff. I repeat: what's your pleasure?"

"The tape, I, I guess." Chris's voice is trembling, and Rob knows why. He hates to ask for what he wants.

"No need to stuff your mouth with that rag I used before. I know it hurts your jaw," says Rob, pressing the tape over Chris's lips, wrapping three layers around his head, cutting the end off, smoothing the gag against his cheeks. "How's that feel?"

It feels wonderful, Chris wants to say. *I'm so scared and so turned on. I am so fucked up. Please take care of me. I need to be saved so bad.* Instead he nods his head.

"Are your hands hurting you?"

Chris grunts *No*.

"Well, before I leave, let me tell you what's in store for you tonight." Rob stands behind Chris, tousling his hair, stroking his bare shoulders, cupping the dense flesh of his pecs in his palms. "Once Mark is here, we're going to cut you loose, tie your hands in front of you so you'll be more comfortable, and help you upstairs. We're going to leave you gagged, Chris. We're going to get you naked, Chris, we're going to shove you down onto your

elbows and knees, and then, Chris, we're going to take turns
fucking your hairy ass, deep and rough, just the way you like it.
We might even work a plug up inside you for the night. Would
you like that?"

Chris gazes at the toy-table, then at the floor, at the dog
sleeping beneath the sling. Slowly he nods. He despises this:
what honey abject helplessness is, how badly he wants his butt
filled up. horny?

"You're going to sleep bound and gagged between us every
night. One of us will be here to take care of you just about
all the time, and the times we're both gone, well, you'll be just
fine down here, won't you?" Rob nods toward the sling, cross,
and paddle-bench. "Isn't this what you've always dreamed of?
To be kidnapped by some big guy and held captive? Don't you
remember confessing that to me when we went camping at Holly
River? The thought turned me on so much, I never forgot."

Rob's standing in front of Chris now, loving his long-
lashed brown eyes, his square jaw, his brown goatee bushing
out beneath the tape; loving his big football-player's shoulders,
tattooed arms, thick pecs, and fuzzy belly bound tightly to the
chair. "God, boy, you're so beautiful like this," Rob mutters.
He drops to his knees, brushes his beard over Chris's very hard
nipples, then takes one into his mouth.

Chris throws back his head and groans. Rob's so, so good
at tit-work. Soon, inevitably, Chris is growling with discomfort,
tossing his head from side to side as Rob does what he always
does with Chris's tits in his mouth: after sucking them hard, he
chews and nips them till they're raw. Now Rob's rubbing the
bulge in Chris's jeans, unzipping them, pulling out his prisoner's short beer can of a cock. He's tying a thin cord around the
base of Chris's dick and balls till they're glossy and swollen.
He's lapping the arrowhead of rigid flesh, reaching up to twist

the sore nipples and caress the chest hair as his hunger bobs in Chris's lap. As heated up as Chris is by his helpless state, it takes him about three minutes to shoot down Rob's throat. It takes another two minutes for Rob to finish, slapping his dick against Chris's gag, pumping himself till a thick spurt lands in the hair between Chris's aching nipples.

Rob's gone now. He's put the cowboy hat back on Chris's head, blown out the candles, left the stereo on. The door is cracked for the dog to lope upstairs if she wants, but it's not a freedom she's interested in. She continues dozing beneath the sling. Chris moves his wrists around in his bonds, gently now, not trying to escape, just reminding himself of how little he has left to decide. His shoulders are stiff, but soon enough his daddies will be back to bind him more comfortably, to make love to him for hours. He needs a big man's weight on him so badly, so badly needs a loving cock up his ass.

The semen Rob shot on his chest is thinning, liquefying, oozing down his belly. How he wants to taste it. Into the tape Chris mumbles *Thank you*, to no one in particular, to dark deepening over these Virginia mountains, to the frantic cheeps of crickets sensing cool nights and searching for cellar warmth, to a distant flash of lightning and purr of thunder, the very storm Rob's been praying for, relief for his parched garden.

Now, more immediate and mechanical thunder, the freight train rumbles by again, going somewhere Chris cannot imagine. This time he is fully awake, this time he hears it rocking noisily along its silvery timeworn tracks. The sound comforts him, the way the purling of brooks does, or the sough of pines, or rain on the roof. As he listens, he strains his mouth against the tape just to feel its tautness over his lips. Where did this contentment come from? How can God disapprove? He's been taken, he's fought to no avail, bigger and stronger men have overpowered him. He never wanted Tammy. He treated her so badly. Instead, Jesus, oh Jesus, he has ached after this: to be forced, to escape free will, to be silent, to be still. How did Rob know? Something is breaking loose in Chris tonight, the exposed earth of clear-cut hillsides sliding into the valley, washing away in brown floodwaters.

He bows his head, sleepy, drained, glad to be alone, glad to know Rob and Mark are driving back through the dark to own him. But before he can drowse, just as the last boxcar rumbles past beyond the cellar wall, the black dog is up and by his side. She wags her tail. Beneath the tape Chris smiles. She circles him. With his bound hands, he reaches out. She stops, nuzzling and licking his fingers. He strokes her muzzle, mumbling *Good dog, good dog.*

Then he's sinking again, into darkness, into approaching thunder, into the rope and tape that are his chrysalis. He will sleep deep tonight, after his nipples and asshole are loved sweet-sore. All night he will be held captive between strength and strength while welcome rain sweeps the hills. Sun will wake him tomorrow, bars of light across his eyes, far-ranging gifts of a star, colors he has never known before. Two lovers will stroke him into rapture, into completion. Two lovers will lift him to his feet.

KEEPING IT UNDER WRAPS

Bill Brent

We don't say a word. We've never met before. Just two horny guys at a sex party. He wanders into an empty room, giving me the come-hither look recognized by horny guys everywhere.

In the room, he is seated on the couch, legs spread, touching himself through the one-piece latex suit covering his trunk. It has short sleeves and legs. This is a rubber fetish party, my first. I feel inadequate in my standard-issue leather vest and Levi's.

I lower my face to his. My intuition is working tonight. I know that he likes being nibbled on the neck—prefers it to sloppy, wet kisses. He writhes beneath me as I press one hand firmly into his pectorals, pinning him down. Now I nip into him more intensely, lips covering teeth. His breathing deepens.

My fingers massage the hot latex suit. There's a zipper down the front. I tug to the spot between his broad pecs, exposing splayed brown hairs. He looks at me with large brown eyes. I kiss him dryly on the mouth. We begin dry-kissing. Our breath is hot.

I reach inside the zipper, kneading and pinching his exposed pectoral flesh. I'm invading him, molesting him. My dick jumps. I notice through his jumpsuit that I'm having the same effect on him. I slide my knee up to his balls and press into him as I pinch his nipples through the latex.

I slap his inner thighs. They're hot from the latex. I remove my vest and pull the front of my black T-shirt over my head and behind my neck, exposing my chest. I place his hands over my largish nipples, and we begin tugging each other's tits, his still covered in latex. I begin slapping them with my hands, pummeling this boy trapped beneath his tight rubber skin.

I take my dick out, rigid now, and slap it against his thighs. It gets so hard, it almost hurts. I pull a small vial of lube from my pocket and squeeze some onto my dick. I jack it off in front of him, slapping the hard cock against my outstretched palm. I open up a rubber and squeeze some lube into it, wiping off my sticky hand and rolling the affair down my swollen shaft. I put it up to his lips, and he hungrily gobbles it down. My knee slides to his groin again. I stroke his fine brown hair.

Most guys don't like to suck on condoms, but for him, it's one more piece of latex fetish. So I pull out a second condom and try to place it around my nuts. This provides some comic relief as I try, then he tries, to trap the stubborn balls. Finally I shrug, giving up, and we laugh a bit.

He looks so hot in that rubber suit. Hot to the touch, too. I squeeze him all over. It's as if he's the last guy I'll ever get to grope and I'm trying to carve this memory into the deepest groove I can find, to make it last a lifetime. Part of me wants to rip him out of his kinky rubber armor, part wants to keep him trapped inside it forever, all tantalizingly displayed and hot to the touch. I squeeze his well-developed biceps and broad, fleshy shoulders; run my fingers through his beautiful hair; squeeze his pointy nipples and his love handles, and finally his hot, hard dick. This time I slap it with the backs of my fingers, gently at first, worried that I'll slap too hard and break the spell. But he likes it, so I slap harder and harder, testing the depth of his limit, and squeezing his ample balls.

Then I hold his balls and gaze intently into his eyes. His nostrils flare. Out of nowhere come the backs of my fingers, slapping him lightly across one cheek. The eyes widen. I kiss him dryly on the mouth. Then again. Slap. Kiss. Slap. Kiss. I feel surges of blood through his balls where I clench them. "Take it out," I hiss. It's the first time either of us has spoken in ten minutes of anonymous sex.

He scrambles to comply, sitting up and beginning to unzip. "Slowly," I say. "Turn me on." I grab my rubberized dick and jack off, pinching my nipples, each of us now showing off for the other.

He slides his fingers down his stomach, teasing the zipper to its end. He gingerly pries his moist cockflesh loose from the clutching rubber sheath, then his balls. He raises his eyebrows, gesturing toward my lube. I hold up the bottle and squeeze some goo onto his fingers. He works it over his expanding dick. I draw closer and slip my hands under the open suit, really working his nipples now. His dick gets enormous—I can't cover it with both my hands. So I hand him a condom.

He extracts it, and I squirt lube into the tip. We unroll it down his sticky dick; it barely reaches bottom. Then I kneel between his knees and take it in my mouth, biting the head between my teeth and tickling his balls. He's working my nipples just the way I like, and soon the whole hot package is throbbing down my throat and I'm biting him on just the other side of the latex tube, down near his nuts. I can tell he's amazed. It's not as if many guys can do this for him. I'm not one of those tops who think that cocksucking is always the role of the bottom. My forceful attitude gets these submissive, big-dicked boys all hot and bothered. I only reveal my champion dickchomper side once their cocks are stiff beyond resistance.

I milk the groaning boy for several minutes with my well-trained throat, and then I begin jacking him off with both hands. He wants lube, so I give him the bottle again, and he starts jacking on my condom-clad cock with his sticky hand. I grab his dick near its base and start slapping it into my palm. I feel a new tension building in his thighs, and as I slap and jerk his dick, I mutter, "Yeah, fucker. That dick's gonna shoot. Gonna fill up the rubber with hot scum. Gonna dump your fat load into that tube. Gonna slap it around till you fuckin' come, Rubber-Boy. Gonna tickle your fat gonads till they squirt for me—"

He knows I've got him trapped till he surrenders. And then he's doing it, twisting and gasping, as I give his boner one final slap. It leaps until the little nipple at the tip of the rubber looks painfully bloated. Through the casing, I tickle him under his ridge until he can't take any more.

I stand, stretching my cramped legs, certain we are through, but then he reaches out and grasps my rubberized dick, still hard from watching his eruption, and jacks me off. Normally this wouldn't blast me off, but I'm so turned on that in two minutes I'm bellowing and spurting my load into that rubber, amazed. My entire body trembles.

We catch our breath, staring at each other and grinning like idiots. Soon we will leave this couch, shed this sticky bondage, and become separated by ever-growing numbers of men, miles, days, years—but right now we're just two blissed-out guys, happy to be together in this room, no longer horny.

MY EIGHTEENTH BIRTHDAY

Larry Townsend

I recently overheard a conversation (I won't tell you where) that brought to mind a similar situation I knew about firsthand. I have to admit taking a bit of poetic license, in that I combined the two accounts into one more titillating whole. At least, I found it titillating.

I was still in high school when I started playing these games. That was a time when I was much more easily embarrassed than I would be today. I was also a lot better looking: slender and well defined, without much body hair—even less after I shaved my pubes to make my cock look bigger. Unlike Dad, I'd been circumcised, but I was more than adequately endowed. Shaving my crotch also made it more convenient when I tied myself up, not to have the knots tangle in the hair around my cock and balls. And that, in essence, is the basis of my adventure. I was a horny teenager, attracted to other guys, but completely at a loss how to make contact, especially since I really wanted someone to render me bound and helpless, and then to use me in a variety of different painful, humiliating ways.

I had never been "abused" or "molested," and maybe my attitude would have been different if I had; but whenever I heard or read about some fiend taking advantage of an innocent young-ster I sprung a steely boner, imagining myself as the recipient of such attentions. My dad was often central to these fantasies, with his hard, rangy body and rugged good looks. But I knew these dreams were no more than flights of wishful thinking. So, with that much as background, let me tell you what really happened.

We lived in a penthouse atop a high-rise. My father was the head of scientific development for a large aerospace firm, the apartment being one of his many perks. My mother had departed the scene several years before, after a rather sedate divorce. Now on his own, Dad usually kept a fairly set schedule, never getting home before six. I usually got home from school around four, so this left me alone in the apartment for a good two hours every afternoon. In the early stages of my activities I stayed pretty much inside my own bedroom. I used to use a heavy clothes-line to tie myself into various exotic positions, my favorite being with my back against the edge of an open closet door. I would run ropes over either side of the panel, using the hinges to keep them from falling. I would then pull them tight across my chest, and up around the neck, where I tied off the rope. Another went around my cock and balls, tied back between my legs, up the crack of my ass and onto the door handles. (Did that ever feel good!) I would fashion noose-loops onto these, and slip my hands through them to simulate a really secure bondage. It took me several tries, but I was eventually able to make myself cum by straining against the ropes and pulling so as to make the bindings tighten around the base of my genitals and against the prostate. After this I'd leave myself tied up until I felt the sensations rebuild. I'd then jack off at a slow, deliberate pace, tantalizing myself just beneath the ultimate until I couldn't stand it any longer, my balls fairly aching for release.

Later, on warm summer evenings, I started going outside onto our terrace after I was sure that Dad was asleep. There were two metal poles set into the deck to support an aluminum awning. These were naturals! Sometimes I'd tie myself against one of them, facing out; other times I'd tie myself front-side toward the post, secured by ropes around my neck and around my balls. Then I'd twist my hands into a tangle of rope behind my back and imagine a wild scenario of being captured by pirates or by some ancient barbarian band. I was secured in public, naked and helpless while the whole gang of brutes looked on. If I imagined myself on a sailing ship, it would be the boatswain who lashed my back with a cat-o'-nine-tails. In the dark forests of the barbarous hordes I'd be whipped with supple wands cut from nearby saplings. These images inevitably brought me off much too quickly, but I soon realized that a few minutes recovery would allow a more leisurely "second cumming." When I finally untied myself there would be a regular pool of jism cooling on the tiles.

Naturally, as time went by, my imagination and my lusting balls drove me to ever wilder and more risky adventures. ("Risky" mostly from the standpoint of possible discovery.) Fear that someone might see me had kept me from playing my games on the terrace during daylight. However, our building was higher than any others in the area, and so far away from any of comparable height that I knew no one could possibly spy on me. Thus I started acting out my nocturnal games on warm, sunny afternoons, during that summer following my high school graduation. I devised a great scenario, whereby I was stretched spread-eagle, standing between the two steel poles. These were about ten feet apart, and each had a vertical row of holes along the side facing the wall, this to permit eyebolts being screwed in to support the bindings for sunshades or other patio niceties. I used them to fasten the ropes that (first) encircled my ankles and stretched my legs wide apart. The ends of these were drawn back from the poles and anchored around my cock and balls. My wrists were similarly secured, with the rope-ends bound tightly around my neck. One arm was secured for real, the other merely wrapped to simulate complete restraint. It was a wild sensation, standing naked and bound in the bright sunlight with the whole city stretched out in front of me, a gentle breeze making the sweat feel cool along the sides of my body.

I had been playing my ever more intricate bondage scenes on the open terrace for a couple of weeks when Dad brought home several surplus items from his office, including some high-tech sound equipment and a multipower telescope. "These were all replaced with new stuff," he explained. "but they're still first-rate."

"Do we get to keep them?"

"I bought the sound equipment," he replied. "The telescope is borrowed, but if you enjoy it we can make it your birthday present." It was then a little over two weeks to my eighteenth.

Dad set the telescope up near the outer edge of the terrace that first night and played with it for a couple of hours before going to bed. He showed me how to adjust the focus and other controls. We were looking skyward, of course, mostly examining the surface of the moon and following the progression of constellations in the zodiac. Because of all this, Dad stayed up well past his usual bedtime. As a result, I almost didn't play my bondage games, fearing that he might be awake longer than usual after going to bed. I needn't have worried; I could hear his heavy breathing less than half an hour after he retired.

So, horny as ever, I crept down the hall naked with a coil of rope in one hand. Then, when I was out on the terrace, I couldn't help wondering about the telescope's potential as an instrument for more earthly discoveries. I pulled the plastic cover off the black steel cylinder and swiveled it around so that it pointed toward the nearest of the distant high-rises. It took some manipulating of the controls, but I was eventually able to focus on the upper-floor windows of a tall, rather narrow brick building.

I was surprised—almost shocked—to realize how close the high-powered lens brought me to my distant neighbors. Most of the inhabitants, like me, must have assumed that their wide separation from any other structures gave them a nearly total privacy. I saw a naked woman step out of the shower, scratching at her private parts as she would never have done had she suspected anyone could observe her movements. I slowly scanned a number of other windows, finding nothing of great interest, and was about to replace the cover when I came to a room that was just dark enough to keep me from seeing into it. But there was some kind of movement just beyond the window, which was open, and this intrigued me. Dad had shown me a control called a "light catcher" that permitted the telescope to concentrate all the available illumination from the huge front lens element and, especially at shorter distances, to see more than the naturally occurring light would have allowed. I fiddled with the controls and eventually turned the focus knob until the vague shadows inside the distant room coalesced into a barely discernable image. It took me a moment to realize it, but I was looking into the business end of another telescope! More than this, the person operating it was obviously male—naked, with a substantial mass of shadow about his groin. I froze in abject terror. This person, this man—whoever he was—he'd been able to see me almost as clearly as if he'd stood on the terrace while I performed my insane rituals. I could feel my prick shrivel in fear and humiliation, and my balls drew up almost into their prepubescent sockets. I hastily replaced the plastic cover on the telescope and fled back inside.

Later, lying in bed, unable to fall asleep, my thoughts became a little more rational. First, it was unlikely that my snooping neighbor could have a telescope as powerful as Dad's. His had been state of the art only a few years ago and had a much higher magnification than any but the most expensive scopes available on the commercial market. My adversary (as I had begun to think of him) would most likely lack the light-concentrating control on his machine that I had on mine. Then I froze again. What if he'd been watching me during the day when light was no problem? The terror returned and I turned over helplessly, lying on my belly and sobbing into the pillow. I was beyond embarrassment. I was mortified! Still, the sensation of my naked body against the sheets was stimulating the old sensations, and gradually I began a peculiar transition into another realm of fantasy. Why would that man want to watch me? He must have found me attractive, interesting at least. If I could enjoy the image of myself being whipped and punished before a crowd of jeering barbarians, why should the idea of another man watching me be so terrifying? Then I went a step further. What if he was turned on by my bound and naked body? What if he was handsome and horny like me? What if he would do the things to me that I desperately wanted, but couldn't do to myself? What if...what if...? And I finally fell asleep.

For the next week I returned to my earlier mode, playing my bondage games in my own room, mostly in the afternoon when I had the apartment to myself. But the combination of lust and curiosity finally overcame my embarrassed reluctance, and

I went naked onto the darkened terrace after Dad was safely tucked in for the night. I hesitated to stand by the edge of the terrace, where Dad had set the telescope. Somehow, moving around at the rear where the poles were located seemed less public. But it was quite dark, with no moon, and I finally got up the courage to uncover the telescope and adjust it. It took me several minutes, but I eventually focused on the same window. This time there was a bit more light, and although the distant telescope stood in the same place, no one was using it. Instead, I could see a portion of the room and several barely discernable forms...discernable, but not definable. I'm sure if I saw them today I'd know what they were, but as an inexperienced almost-eighteen-year-old, I wasn't sure. What little light there was must have been coming from several candles, standing just outside my range of vision. It tended to flicker and made it more difficult to know exactly the form inside the area framed by that open window. The real problem, of course, was that I could not believe what I was seeing.

Standing in the middle of the room was a framework—wood? metal? I couldn't tell—consisting of two A-frames with a horizontal pole connecting them at the top. That much I could believe. But stretching my credibility was the still, unmoving figure that seemed to be suspended from the center of the crossbar. I thought it was a slender, well-muscled man with a black hood over his head and several dark bands forming a cross against his chest and a heavy belt around his waist. His hands were apparently joined together behind his back, where I couldn't see them. I kept staring, readjusting the focus on the telescope, but I was unable to make the picture any clearer. Although my conscious mind continued to question the evidence of my senses, my cock had sprung to full attention; I could feel a fierce, aching warmth engulf my balls and my groin. I must have watched for more than five minutes, but the bound figure (if that was truly what I saw) seemed never to move. Then, quite unexpectedly, there was a dark shadow by the distant telescope. I could only see the vague outline of a man's body as he hunched over his instrument. But he obviously saw me! He stood up straight and stepped back a pace or so, enough that the candlelight reflected off the corded definition of his midsection. One hand stole to his crotch, grasped his cock and pulled on it, stretched the foreskin down. After another moment he released his rod so that it sprang back to point its steely hardness in my direction. He continued to toy with himself for at least three or four minutes, finally taking another step backward, allowing the feeble light to give me a better sight of his firm, extraordinary build.

He permitted me another brief span to admire his physical perfection before reaching behind him and retrieving an object from the wall rack. He looked in my direction, then, and held up a multitailed whip for me to see before he swung it against the back of the tightly bound figure. He lashed his writhing captive for perhaps five minutes before turning to face me, holding up the whip in one hand and beckoning me with the other. He stepped back to his telescope and peered through it in my direction once again, still making the unmistakable motion with his free hand. He was summoning me, commanding me to attend him.

I had gone weak in the knees by this time, my body actually quaking as if I were responding to a sudden chill. But I was anything but cold! Never, not even during my wildest flights of fancy, had I ever been so completely possessed by blind desire, by such an urgent, furious need to seek sexual release—this in a form that lay beyond my ability to describe.

As I watched, he stepped once more into the area beside his captive figure. He unfastened the coupling above the other's head and brought the hooded servitor to his knees. I could see him make some adjustment to the hood before he pressed it into his groin. He was obviously forcing the captive to suck him off, and the thought of this raised my own level of need beyond any reasonable control. I tried to keep watching through the telescope, but this forced me into an impossibly uncomfortable posture. Finally I stood up, bringing back the distant images to my mind's eye, and jacked off until I had cum and cum again. Still holding my half-risen cock in one hand, feeling the fluid as it continued to ooze from the tip, I bent again to peer through the eyepiece. The window was dark; there was nothing more to see. I watched for quite a while, idly stroking myself back to a bloated hardness, my hand gliding along the slickness of my previous ejaculations until I had to stand again and shoot a final blast of passion onto the cool tiles of the terrace. After this I stood at the edge of the deck, naked and still aflame, gazing out over the glitter of city lights, but aware only of the darkened window that I could barely locate with just my bare eyes.

Once I got to bed my cock remained hard. I jacked off again, but it didn't help; I was just as horny as I'd been before. My balls actually ached and I didn't fall asleep until after daylight seeped in around my bedroom curtains. It was Saturday, also my eighteenth birthday. I got up around noon, feeling as if I'd been drugged the night before. But once I stumbled into the shower I began to regain my equilibrium, and by the time I finished I was ready for the next stage of my adventure. I knew that I had to find my "adversary," that it was unlikely he would come to me. There was a note for me on the kitchen table: Dad had to attend a conference at the office, but he'd be home by six to take me out for a special holiday treat. I had some juice and a roll, then sitting over coffee I studied a city map. The building I sought was in an older area, one I had never needed to visit. I managed to figure out the probable street name, as well as the most likely intersections. I also gazed through the telescope again to fix the building's contour more firmly in my mind.

Once I reached the general area, I had no trouble finding the right address. It was an old office building that had been converted into a series of trendy lofts. The front door wasn't locked, but the big, rickety elevator required a key to operate. There were several call buttons, but they were coded, with no reference to which floor they would reach. I was standing in the big, flagstone foyer, wondering what to do next when a young guy came in. At first glance he did not seem exceptional, wearing a pair of heavy, dark-rimmed glasses that gave him an owlish look. He was slender, though, and obviously well muscled beneath the baggy, somewhat scruffy jeans and cut-off sweatshirt. He gave me a cursory glance before pressing one of the buttons. When he reached out to insert his key I noticed a red circle imbedded in the skin of his wrist, and a couple of fading bruises higher up on his arm. I could hear the elevator rumbling down and knew I had only a moment if I was going to say anything. He was obviously not the man I had seen at the telescope, but he might well have been the hooded figure I had seen in the background.

I cleared my throat, which caused him to glance up at me. "I...I was wondering," I managed. "Are you...ah, going to the top floor?"

"Yeah, I am. What's it to ya?"

"Ah...I think I was...with you last night."

He stared at me, then, a blank look at first, followed by a crooked grin. "Telescope?"

"Yeah."

"Come on," he said, motioning me into the elevator. "I thought I recognized you," he added as the slatted door creaked shut. "I'm Roy," he told me.

"I'm Alex," I replied

After these brief introductions we rode up in silence. I'm sure my face burned red with embarrassment, imagining how much of my secret world he must have observed. When we reached the top floor and the elevator jolted to a stop, he motioned me back as the gate swung open. He took off his glasses and started to strip. "If you want to come in, you have to be naked. Only the Master wears clothes in the workshop."

I hesitated to follow his lead, although he was completely stripped in a matter of seconds, naked except for his white sweat socks. He leaned against the wall to remove these, giving me a full view of his denuded crotch; like mine, closely shaved to better display a long dangling cock and deep full sac. Needless to say, I was totally enflamed. He, on the other hand, seemed completely unconcerned to be so exposed. Despite my earlier assessment, he had a beautiful body, and actually a handsome face now that those ugly glasses had been removed. The sight of him in this condition had aroused more than just my interest, as evidenced by the desperate rise and pressure in my crotch. I was still frozen in a state of disbelief—not that I was adverse to the idea; it just seemed too good to be true. Seeing that I was reluctant to follow his lead, he shrugged. "It's up to you," he said. "Strip and come in with me, or I'll send you back down."

I stripped. Roy placed his neatly folded clothes on a bench beside the elevator, motioning for me to do the same. Then he took hold of my bloated, half-risen cock and led me into the foyer of the loft.

I sensed that the pressure of the young man's fingers about my cock marked some ultimate symbol of my surrender, and of entering into a new, totally unknown realm. I had never been touched like this before, and except for a few tantalizing memories of the boys' shower room, I had never shared such total nakedness with another guy, certainly not in this highly charged, sexual context. I was so aroused it was almost overwhelming. I moved inside an aura of my own body heat—sweating, I realized, although the temperature was comfortable. Roy led me to an ironbound wooden door, set into an otherwise solid wall that appeared to be stone. He lifted a heavy wolf's head knocker, tapping it gently against the panel. His request was answered by a soft buzzing sound and a substantial "click" that caused the door to swing inward.

I don't know what I'd expected, but only my wildest flights of fancy might have prepared me for this room. Along a narrow, dimly lighted corridor that must have run the entire width of the building was a continuous row of cell doors...perhaps a dozen in total. They were made of heavy mesh, like a chain-link fence, and the nearest two seemed occupied by naked figures who sat cross-legged on the stone floor. Standing in the center of the corridor to my left was a big, powerfully built man wearing what appeared to be a brown leather apron. He was naked except for this and a skullcap of the same material and some sort of soft rough-out boots. His arms were crossed against his chest. He looked like some medieval dungeon master. Roy had finally let go of my prick and taken a few steps back. This left me alone to face the Master. My gaze kept moving from him to the caged prisoners and back, fear beginning to mingle with awe as I tried to accept a reality that was so bizarre, yet so completely in keeping with my fantasies that I might almost have constructed it all from my secret mental images.

"We have a few hours to wait," said the Master, without further elaboration. His voice was soft, almost soothing, although it was of a deep, dark-toned timbre. He motioned toward the nearest empty cell, and Roy led me into it...not touching me until we were both inside. Then he took hold of my shoulders, turned me to face a width of screen beside the door, and guided me to stand against it. The Master stood watching us, silent as Roy went about his work. He positioned me with arms and legs spread wide, apparently taking his unspoken instructions from the Master, who remained in front of me, nodding occasionally until his minion had me posed as he required. He then reached behind him and took a handful of rawhide strips from a peg in the outer wall. Deftly, without a wasted motion, he secured my wrists to the mesh, while Roy knelt in back of me and did the same with my ankles. Once I was firmly secured, the Master stepped back and Roy came out to join him. At another nod from the commanding figure, Roy reached inside the mesh and pulled my genitals through one of the openings.

I was bound, I realized, in much the same posture I had assumed during some of my own solo games, except that I was now genuinely restrained and my struggles were something more than pretense. The Master grinned as if pleased—at least satisfied—and turned to leave. "You may enjoy yourselves," he said simply, and closed the heavy door behind him.

The whole vault was silent for a minute, so still that I could hear the blood rushing through my veins; my heart seemed to be pounding inside my skull. Then Roy moved up to seize my cock, still half-hard despite my growing fear and the tenseness that was already creeping into my arms and shoulders. He played with me, licking his lips, moving his face closer to mine as if he intended to kiss me. But the mesh separated us. Still I pressed my face against it and Roy's seeking tongue probed into me. I could feel the heat welling up in my balls and I tried to pull away, not wanting to shoot my load.

To help regain control I sought to distract myself long enough for my lusts to lose their focus. "The others," I whispered. "Are you going to free them?" I could hear some shuffling sounds from the neighboring cells, as their occupants were apparently trying to observe us.

Roy laughed softly. "It's the weekend," he explained. "They come to us on Friday night and they remain in custody until Monday...sometimes a little longer."

I wasn't sure I understood his meaning, but my own needs took over. I tried again to kiss him, but this time he went down on his knees and took my cock into his mouth. Just the touch of him, the warmth, the moisture...it brought the fluids boiling out of my balls, cascading down my shaft to fill him, catching him momentarily off guard so that he choked at the initial onslaught. He swallowed all I could give him, but never relinquished his hold. He knew I was good for another blast, and maybe something beyond that. He knew because he'd watched me, I thought, and for just a moment the sense of embarrassment, or betrayal, made me lose a modicum of hardness. But almost immediately I was back in stride, driving myself into him, demanding as best I could in my total bondage until I delivered another bolt.

I was not taken down for a long time, and was left alone for much of the afternoon as Roy visited a couple of the other cells. Only three were occupied by "weekenders," I discovered, although there were apparently a pair of long-term captives in the cubicles on either end of the passage. Roy never went near these; in fact he had a substantial interaction only with the guy in the cell one down from me. I couldn't see, of course, but I could hear an intriguing rattle of chains and the sharp impact of leather on flesh. There were groans and cries of pain, muted finally when Roy apparently gagged his subject. Except for the involuntary outcries no one spoke, and an eerie silence seemed to engulf the entire prison. Silence must have been the rule, I thought, some regulation imposed by the Master.

I had no way to tell how long I had been spread-eagle against the mesh, but I ached through my entire body; the rawhide bindings were cutting into my wrists and ankles; and worst of all, I had to piss. Finally, Roy finished his games in the other cell and came back to check on me. He felt my hands and feet, testing to assure I sustained no serious harm. "Please let me down," I whispered. "I really gotta piss."

He reached in and touched my face with his fingers, pressing one into my mouth so that I could suck on it. Then he knelt in front of me as he had before and took my swollen, tumescent prick into his mouth. I could see his face tilted up to meet my own gaze, and I thought he made a slight nodding motion. His lips tightened on my shaft, and I could feel him pulling on it. I could hardly believe that he wanted me to piss into his mouth, but I was to a point where I could not hold on much longer. I released a small trickle and felt him press more firmly into my groin. Then I let go, flooding him with my piss, which he took for several heartbeats before slipping free and bending his head beneath the warm cascading rush. His hair was soaked as he leaned back, allowing the full blast to gush across his face and down the front of his supplicating body. In the end it formed a rivulet down the center of his chest, into his groin, and along his own cock to spill into a steaming puddle on the floor about his knees.

He took me down a little while later and sponged me off with a cloth soaked in warm, slightly scented water. He gave me some beer to drink, which made me a little woozy, and some plain saltine crackers. After this we sat together on a wooden bench in the hall outside my cell until the Master returned. In all that time, I'm sure that Roy had never made any attempt to dry himself or to otherwise wipe my piss from his hair and body.

I was taken into the same room that I had watched through the telescope and placed under the double *A*-frame. Leather cuffs were locked around my wrists, and a leather hood was placed over my head. Banks of candles guttered in groups from the corners of the chamber. It had been dark outside when we entered the room, although I don't think it was very late. It occurred to me that I should have been home long before now, or should at least have called. Now it was too late. The hood had a wide leather flap that fit into my mouth and effectively gagged me. There was also a snap-on piece across my eyes, intended to act as a blindfold. However, one side had come loose and I was able to see a bit, mostly the front of my own body and my feet until these were seized and pulled wide apart, bound to either side of the frame. This left me suspended, hanging by my wrists.

I was not in any real pain, not yet. The leather cuffs were padded and kept anything from cutting into me. I could hear Roy talking to the Master, their whispered words partially muffled by my hood. I thought they were doing something with their telescope, and twice I was sure I heard Roy call the Master "Daddy." There was a soft burring, ringing, like a cell phone, and the Master seemed to answer. But he must have stepped out of the room, because I couldn't hear him for several minutes. At length, after a short, whispered exchange with Roy, they unfastened my ankles from the sides of my frame, allowing me a momentary respite to stand and thus relieve the pressure on my wrists. Then, abruptly, both legs were lifted, and my body was bent double as they hefted my ankles up, against the crossbar. They snapped clamps onto the leather bindings and I was suddenly hanging by my four extremities.

I heard the Master laugh, a soft chuckle, then again, and I realized he must be speaking into his phone. "Chuck says it's a great view of the kid's asshole," he said. I heard him laugh again. "Yeah, eighteen's the game," he added.

Chuck? Chuck was my father's name. I twisted my body, but

I was completely helpless, hanging like a carcass in a slaughterhouse. Then a warm hand came down against my groin, kneading my balls, pulling at my dick. I had grown soft through all of this, and I was trying to think. I had been led into some kind of planned scenario, and now I was completely at the mercy of Roy and his Master—father? I wanted to cry out, to question their intent...question my circumstances. But there was nothing I could do. I was hanging by my wrists and ankles, supported by a waistband, unable to make any move to protect myself. Worse, I could feel the motion of air against my asshole, and was doubly embarrassed to realize that my most private area was openly displayed, vulnerable for whatever use either of my captors might wish to make of it. Gently, the unseen hand began to manipulate my prick, to caress it, knead it, one finger playing about the tip until I knew I had released a few drops of precum, felt the fingers play with it, rub it onto my cockhead, and continue teasing me back to total hardness. Finally, while the taunting hand continued its ministrations, a second began to explore my asshole. I started at the unexpected touch, but had no choice, no way to resist or even protest. I forced myself to relax the muscles as one long, probing digit entered me, spreading a sensation of warmth. It was coated with something slick, slippery. I groaned, and tried to lift myself away from the invading contact. But the possession continued until I accepted it, hung slack in my bondage and ceased my futile attempt to resist.

No one had spoken through all of this, but I knew it had to be Roy who manipulated me. His cock was pressing against me, trying to ease its way inside, sliding easily through the lubricated passage. He went slowly, never forced himself, and gradually my body accommodated his entry. He had continued to massage my cock, causing such a flood of sensation I hardly reacted to the brief, sharp stab of pain when he fully penetrated me. I was lost in the most thoroughly encompassing wave of pleasure I had ever known, and this simply mounted in intensity as he began slowly pumping himself into me, then out, and back again. I was experiencing the kind of penetration I had only dreamed of. I had always been afraid to poke anything into myself, so this was my first anal experience. It was certainly everything I had ever imagined it would be, and I was still riding this emotional high when I felt the hood being loosed and gradually pulled from my head.

At first, even the dim illumination made me blink, and it took another moment to focus my gaze. I saw Roy standing against me, grasping my thighs as he continued to fuck my ass. The Master stood to one side watching us, and next to him was my dad! If I had not been in such a state of physical euphoria I would surely have freaked. But Roy leaned harder against me, forcing his cock to its fullest depth. He touched my lips with his, then drew back and whispered "Happy Birthday!" before plunging his tongue fully into my mouth. It was another few minutes before the full truth dawned on me. Eighteen was indeed the key, or more precisely the threshold, to adulthood...an initiation, a rite of passage...the most incredible milestone I would ever celebrate.

IN THE HEAT OF THE NIGHT

Jay Starre

C lay rode just behind RC. Out since dawn, they now followed along the left bank of a quiet stream that meandered through the vast emptiness of the eastern Colorado prairie. It was nearing sunset, and ahead, a bank of clouds broiled on the distant horizon.

The summer heat was oppressive. Sweat dribbled down Clay's armpits and sides. His crotch was sopping and slipped uncomfortably where he sat in his saddle. The raging boner rubbing against his shorts and the inside of his jeans fly didn't help.

RC was the reason for that hard-on. Blond, green eyed, and quiet, the ranch boss was a real hunk of cowboy. Clay had hinted on numerous occasions that he was hot for him, but RC hadn't taken the bait.

Yet here they were, alone in the eastern pastures. RC had ordered Clay to accompany him on the fence-line inspection. They were camping out on the range that night, just the two of them.

Clay's hard-on throbbed as he stared hungrily at the broad back above the muscular butt spread over the saddle of RC's bay mare. He'd fuck that ass if he could. He'd do any nasty thing RC wanted if he could.

Clay, auburn haired, barely twenty-one, with bright golden eyes and a carefree chatty nature, did practically all of the talking on that long summer day, as they rode for miles under the summer sky, stopping at times to replace broken wire or reposition loose fence posts. "This looks like a good spot to camp, RC. We can sneak under the cover of those willows if that thunderstorm makes it this far."

RC turned in his saddle. A rare smile, a nod, and that was it. They camped by a willow copse beside the burbling stream.

Unfortunately, the heat didn't ease appreciably with the sunset. The promise of rain, even though it was likely to come in the form of a drenching thunderstorm, remained far to the west across endless grasslands.

Clay's prick was half-hard throughout the hour it took to set up camp and fry up a meal of steak and 'taters. Lurid fantasies of sucking RC's cock or bending over for the husky cowboy and taking it up the ass roiled through Clay's fevered brain, much like the thunderclouds moving over the far-off mountains.

How could he tempt RC into sex? Could he come right out and suggest something? He didn't want to alienate the big cowboy. But while they ate, Clay, never one to remain silent for long, blabbered on about anything that came to mind, until finally, he blurted it out.

"I'm so damn horny! All this riding and heat and all. How about you, RC? Got a boner tonight?"

His words hung in the air above their campfire like smoke that just wouldn't dissipate. Clay flushed pink and waited with pounding heart for RC's reaction.

RC smiled. A slow grin, enough to display his straight white teeth. Clay held his breath.

"Get over in front of that big willow. Shuck your clothes. Except your boots."

Clay bounded up from his seat on a log and practically tripped over himself as he hastened to obey the quiet command. His mind raced, while his tongue just couldn't stop wagging.

"You want me naked, RC? Butt naked? Sure! I don't mind at all. It's so fucking hot out here anyway! Are you gonna get naked too? If you want, I can jerk you off, if you're horny and all like me. Or whatever you want."

By this time Clay found his spot beneath the overhanging branches of a large willow tree and managed to tear off his shirt and hop out of his pants, yanking one boot off at a time before stepping back into them. Now he was naked except for them, and his white cotton underwear.

His stiff dick tented the skivvies, and he was momentarily embarrassed. His hands hesitated at the waistband as he gazed at RC, who was standing in front of him. A silent nod and a quiet stare was all Clay got, but it was enough. He yanked his underwear down and off over the boots, his cock rearing out in front of him in all its plump glory.

"Turn around. Kneel down."

The words were uttered in the quiet, calm voice RC always employed. Clay whirled on his feet and obeyed, his bare knees settling into the prairie sod, soft here beneath the shade of the willows and beside the stream.

"Are you gonna fuck me up the ass?" Clay blurted.

RC moved away behind Clay, his quiet stride barely discernible among the gathering night sounds. In his breathless state and straining to hear what RC was doing, Clay was all too aware of those noises; crickets and toads, the piercing cry of a nighthawk, the crackling of their campfire, the soft whinnying of their hobbled horses.

"RC? What are you doing?"

Clay was afraid to look back over his shoulder, thinking somehow he'd spoil this unbelievable opportunity. Waiting for RC to answer and hearing him approach again, Clay was totally aware of his nakedness. His knees were wide apart, his asscrack open to the heat of the night. His asshole twitched. And his stiff cock banged up against his navel. He shivered with sudden, intense anticipation.

"Raise your arms. Put your wrists together."

Clay obeyed instantly, his thoughts still on his bare, spread ass, aware of RC standing between his splayed boots. Before Clay realized what was happening, he was trussed.

He gasped. "You're tying me up? With your reins? Then what? What are you gonna do to me?"

The thin leather was supple and smooth from constant use and liberal coatings of oil. RC took good care of his gear. The blond cowboy had snaked the length of leather around Clay's upraised wrists snugly before looping the ends around an over-hanging branch. Clay was now kneeling naked with his wrists bound and his arms stretched toward the willow tree above.

He was helpless.

An intense heat coursed through Clay. His cock jerked against his belly. His asshole clenched nervously. Then RC leaned against him from behind, his calloused palms sliding slowly down Clay's upraised, muscular arms. The rough palms found Clay's armpits and lightly stroked them, sending a wracking shiver through his body.

RC's crotch pressed against the back of Clay's neck, and he felt the unmistakable bulge of stiff cock throbbing through the burly cowboy's jeans. Clay gasped again before RC moved back.

"I'll do whatever you want, RC! I'll suck you off or let you fuck my ass. Whatever you want, boss." Clay whimpered, realizing that he didn't have much choice. RC could do what he liked; Clay was defenceless. Did he know RC, really? For the past year he'd worked with RC, and hungered for some kind of physical contact with the handsome cowboy. But this?

RC was back. His warm breath wafted against Clay's naked shoulder blades. Hands suddenly reached up between Clay's parted thighs. Another length of leather snaked around the base of Clay's stiff cock, scooping up his balls at the same time. A few snug twists and Clay's goodies were hog-tied. The ends of the reins pulled back and down, parted and then, one at a time, wrapped around the ankles of his boots.

The leather stretched tight. He couldn't move his feet in any direction or the reins would pull backward on his bound cock and balls. He really was hog-tied.

The auburn-haired cowboy had only a moment to comprehend what had happened to him before he suffered another, even more intimate assault on his senses.

"What are you doing? God! What's happening to my ass? What are you doing to my hole?" Clay moaned to the branches above his head.

Something stroked his asshole right in the center where it pouted outward, nervous and expectant. He clenched his sphincter, squeezing his ass-lips together briefly, before that tantalizing stroking had him arching his back and gasping, his anal muscles bulging out.

He felt the restraints around his wrists, smelled the leather reins dangling down in his face. He wanted so badly to reach back and feel what was happening to his asshole, but couldn't. He had no choice but to accept it. Whatever it was.

RC laughed, a low chuckle that rumbled within his broad

chest. Suddenly, the awesome hole-stroking stopped, and in front of Clay's face, an object appeared. In the flickering light of the fire, Clay just made out what he was looking at: RC's quirt—a riding whip with trailing, entwined thongs of leather.

Clay gasped. "Are you going to shove it up inside me? Are you going to fuck me with it before you fuck me with your big cock?"

That blurted string of questions was answered by another low rumble of dry chuckles. RC didn't bother answering as the quirt disappeared and a moment later the lazy tickling of Clay's pouting asshole began again.

Clay squirmed. He heaved his ass back against the incessant stroking, wanting now more than anything to be invaded, impaled, fucked by the husky cowboy who had tied him to a tree, at his mercy.

"Do you want it?" The quiet drawl vibrated in Clay's left ear. RC's hot breath played on Clay's neck, the masculine smell of denim and leather and sweat assailing Clay's flaring nostrils.

"Do I want it? Fuck, yeah! I want your cock up my ass, hard and harder! Fuck me, cowboy! Please!"

The breathless plea echoed in the night, punctuated by a distant rumble of thunder. Clay's need intensified. It was going to rain. A storm was coming; he could smell it. He wanted to get fucked before they were drenched in a downpour and their fun and games would have to come to an end. Or would they? Maybe RC would fuck Clay regardless, lightning all around, cock pounding his hungry ass...

The sleek handle of the quirt was back, centered between Clay's distended butt-lips. Slippery fingers rubbed around it, teasing his aching flesh. The quirt slid in, slowly, barely. Fingers lubed Clay's asshole with something. Lard from their stores? The quirt pushed deep into Clay's guts.

"Oh, my god! Oh, yeah! I fucking love it! Uhhhhhhh! More!"

RC obliged, the greased leather handle pushing in deeper and deeper, pulling quickly out, sliding oh-so-steadily back in. Clay squirmed. He bucked. He raised his ass to take the leather rod with eager, quaking swallows of his throbbing ass-lips. The restraints pulled against his ankles and his cock and balls. He could only move so far!

"Sweet. Nice," RC murmured.

Clay was all too aware of how he must look. His pale, hairless ass gleaming in the firelight. Big firm cheeks spread wide with his knees planted far apart to display a deep crack. Narrow waist, tanned broad back rising to broader shoulders. Boots digging into the grass, naked thighs tensed, hamstrings bulging. Leather reins looped around his dangling 'nads and stiff cock, snaking back like the tight strings on a bow to wrap around his boots. Quirt sliding in and out of his greased asshole, dark leather into alabaster ass. And him moaning, writhing, loving this lurid, nasty dream come true.

He could do no more than accept, and submit.

Clay blurted out his thoughts, as usual. "Do whatever you want to me, RC! I'm all yours. My sweet ass is all yours!"

RC removed the quirt with a lazy tug. His greased hole oozed lard, his round ass heaved.

"Are you going to fuck me up the ass, hard, with that huge prick of yours? God, I want it so bad, RC! Please do me—"

Clay's words were cut off as cockhead thrust between his plump lips. RC had stripped down to his boots in less than a minute. His tree-trunk thick, hairy thighs pressed into Clay's head from the side and his cock pushed into the kneeling boy's gaping mouth. That broad plum knob pumped against Clay's tongue and cheeks, seeking his throat.

Clay opened wide, leaning into the reins that bound his wrists, the sturdy branch above easily taking his weight. He relaxed into the mouth-fuck, his head swimming, his throat opening. Prick crown slithered beyond his tonsils, his lips caressing the root of RC's massive shank.

Clay was in paradise, the masculine stench of the cowboy he worshipped surrounding him. RC pulled back a moment to allow Clay a snort of air through his flared nostrils, then while he returned to pumping Clay's throat with lazy, deep lunges, his hands massaged and explored Clay's naked ass. Those rough palms kneaded the chunky globes, pulled them apart, delved between. Blunt fingers stroked the greased anal entrance, tickling and probing as Clay gurgled around the cock buried in his throat.

The young cowboy surrendered to the sensations bombarding him. His booted feet were pulled snug against the reins restraining them, his balls aching with the pressure. His arms went limp, cradled by the reins around his wrists, secure in the strength of the bow above.

RC felt the slack acceptance and slid his cock from Clay's smacking lips. "Time to fuck you, cowboy. Your ass is mine."

The soft-spoken promise sent a wave of expectation coursing up and down Clay's spine. The giant cock he'd just been sucking pressed briefly against his cheek as a pair of fingers dug around in his tender asshole and stretched it open for what was to come.

"Please! Yes! I want you to fuck me! I've wanted it for a year! This is a dream come true for me, RC!" Clay blabbered as RC knelt in the grass between Clay's spread legs.

Prick, wet with spit, rubbed up into his parted crack, gooey with grease. Rough fingers held his smooth asscheeks apart. The hairless mounds quivered with expectation.

Cock rubbed up and down the crack, turgid and heated like

a fat pipe just removed from a blazing furnace. Clay mewled, arching his back, pushing out with his sphincter as the fat shank pressed against his hole.

"Put it in! Fuck me please, RC!" Clay begged.

Broad crown centered on Clay's pulsing anal target. The blunt meat hesitated for just a moment as sphincter quaked around it. Then it rammed deep, impaling Clay in a balls-deep penetration.

"Goddamn!!!!! I am so fucked! Your...prick...is...so...far... up...my....ass!"

RC leaned in to tickle Clay's neck with his tongue. Clay jerked in his bonds as cock yanked all the way out, paused for a breathtaking instant, then slammed home again with a loud smack of naked hips against naked ass.

"Oh! Yes! Ummmnnnn! So good! So hard! Give it to me, cowboy!" Clay cried out enthusiastically as RC pummeled him from behind while sucking on his neck with wet slurps.

The restraints that bound Clay became boundaries he tested and clung to as RC savagely rammed his ass with his pile-driver prick. Relentlessly, in and out, faster and faster the cowboy slammed him as Clay hung from the tree above and took it, his own cock stiff and drooling between his thighs, leather tight around his balls and boots.

Clay didn't know how long it lasted. He cried out nonstop until his voice grew hoarse. His asshole accepted the pounding with aching glee. His body rocked back and forth. The sound of thunder in the distance grew closer, then retreated.

"I'm coming!"

The words hissed in Clay's ear just as that savage cock withdrew from his pummeled asshole. Clay felt warm spunk splatter his left asscheek as prick rubbed all over it. RC held his cock against that lush mound as he coated the bound cowboy with his nut-juice.

Clay felt his own orgasm pulsing on the edge of culmination, but not quite reaching it. His bound balls throbbed, his bound cock pulsed, his fucked asshole quivered.

Then RC rose and abandoned him. The tantalizing promise of release subsided.

"I'll get back to you later, cowboy."

That was all RC said. Clay hung limp, his heart pounding, his lungs heaving. He had never felt so fucked.

The thunder approached, lightning lit up the sky. The smell of rain permeated the air, along with the stink of RC all over Clay.

But it didn't rain, and the storm retreated back toward the west, still threatening,

Clay waited, expectant, on edge. His asshole ached. He wanted to reach back and touch it, stroke it, feel the swollen lips that RC had tenderized with his fat cock. But he couldn't, bound as he was. His cock drooped, then stiffened, in the night's unrelenting heat.

He dozed off, woke to the sound of night creatures and distant thunder still booming. A hand settled on his neck and stroked it.

"RC? Are you gonna fuck me again? I want your cock up my ass! It feels so damn good. I want you to fuck me until I shoot! Can you fuck a load out of me, please?"

RC didn't answer, merely sliding in behind Clay and kneeling between his spread thighs. Cockhead, firm and hot, settled between Clay's swollen butt-lips and began to slide inward.

This time RC fucked Clay with gentle, steady probes. The big cowboy pushed halfway in, then backed out a little, sliding deeper until his furry balls nestled in Clay's hairless crack, holding there for an endless moment, meat pulsing deep in the boy's guts.

It went on and on. Clay merely succumbed to the gentle

probing at first, swaying in his bonds. Then, helplessly, he felt his own excitement mount. His prostate ached from the constant pressure of cock rubbing inside. His ass-lips throbbed with the gentle massaging of RC's big tool. Clay's dick swelled, ached, pulsed against the leather reins surrounding the thick base. His balls ached.

He couldn't stop himself. He writhed and bucked against RC. He arched his back and slammed his ass back. He pulled against his bonds, squirming and moaning.

"Oh, god! Your cock up my ass is so fucking good! I need to shoot! I want to shoot! I need you to fuck me!"

He was there again, on the verge, his entire body straining against his bonds. He felt orgasm coming—

RC withdrew.

"I'll be back."

That was all the big cowboy said as Clay dangled from his bonds and grunted his disappointment. For once, he was at a loss for words. His cock throbbed, swollen and aching. He was a limp rag of sweat and lust hanging from a willow tree in the hot night.

Rain roused Clay from a feverish half-sleep. He straightened as the first fat drops blew sideways against his shoulders. Ah, so cool! He blinked the sleep from his eyes. Dawn neared.

More rain splashed against his naked body. The overhanging willows protected him from the deluge from above, but the prairie gusts slashed sideways to splatter him. He inhaled the moist air, the sweat that coated him washing away.

Memories of the awesome night surfaced, vivid and nasty. His cock stiffened to throb helplessly at his waist. Where was RC? Would he fuck Clay again, or release him?

Clay absorbed the cool rain with an exultant shiver. Whatever happened now, it didn't matter. He'd been fucked, and fucked good! Yet, there was a hefty load still backed up in his balls. He needed to shoot.

Then, he felt it: RC's tongue on his asshole. Wet stabs tested the pouting sphincter, tickled the swollen entrance.

"Oh, god! Yeah! Eat my poor ass, RC! Please! I love it!" Clay called out, his voice husky from overuse.

RC spread Clay's hefty butt wide apart with his big hands. He was on his back in the sod, his face rising up into the open ass valley, his mouth and tongue busy on Clay's hole. Amidst the wind and the spattering raindrops, Clay could hear nasty smacks and slurps as the blond ranch boss really began to munch on cowboy butthole.

The sensation of wet tongue and sucking lips attacking his tender hole sent a wave of lust rocking up and down Clay's bound body. He arched his back, squatted over RC's face and relaxed into his bonds. He swayed limply, rocking over the wet face and stabbing tongue.

He surrendered totally, his ass wide open, his head hanging down, his stiff cock drooling nonstop as his asshole gaped open to an oral assault that seemed to stab right up into his guts and lungs.

"Eat my ass! Oh, yeah! Tongue my hole! Oh…god…I fucking love it, RC! My hole is all yours!"

Clay's moans and gasps battled with the earsplitting crash of thunder. Brilliant lightning illuminated the scene, outlining in stark clarity the bound cowboy spread wide over the cowboy's face that held his ass open and tongued the palpitating hole so expertly.

Clay went totally limp. His mouth hung open, his arms dangling from the reins trapping his wrists. Waves of pleasure cascaded up his body from that sucking mouth and stabbing tongue.

Then, one of RC's rough hands seized Clay's stiff cock. The calloused palm pumped up and down while tongue probed pouting hole. It was sudden and it was too much.

"I'm shooting! Oh...my...fucking...god!"

Clay, dangling from his restraints, a tongue probing his hole, spewed a load of sticky semen over the prairie sod between his spread legs. Tongue continued to tickle and stab as his balls released their pent-up load. His body rocked and vibrated within his restraints.

All at once, he was being released. RC had moved with characteristic silent swiftness. Reins untwined from Clay's wrists; a moment later, they slipped off his boots and then dropped away from his still spurting dick.

Rough hands raised him up on shaky legs and burly arms enveloped him in an embrace. Clay moaned as he settled against RC's naked body, dribbling the last of his load and barely able to breathe.

Dawn arrived in full force just then, the rain clouds moving off to the west, the sky magenta and vermilion.

Totally unexpectedly, RC leaned down and kissed Clay. The young cowboy sighed, and for once, had nothing to say.

STRAIGHT AS A QUESTION MARK

Len Richmond

A lone on New Year's Day, I scan through a list on a long yellow legal pad. It carefully notes the names, ages, and sexual fantasies of all the men who left me *L.A. Weekly* voice mails.

The thirteenth on my list claims he's "very curious, very hot, and very handsome." A straight young actor who's interested in acting out his "bottom fantasies" with another man.

My nervous new "bottom" shows up an hour late for our date (not unusual). He says his name is Jeff, but I doubt it. On the list of forty-four names there are five "Jeffs," eight "Ricks," twelve "Johns," and thirteen "Marks." Simple names, I suppose, so they can remember their aliases.

Jeff is so scared he keeps staring down at his hands (or is it his crotch?) as we sit on the couch. Whenever we do have fleeting eye contact, he giggles nervously. As he peels the label off his second bottle of beer, strip by strip, the metaphor of his movements is becoming abundantly clear. Without saying it, he's shouting, "My sexuality's all bottled up and I can't wait to peel my clothes off!"

He's awful cute. Six foot two and eyes of blue. Muscular body and a sweet shy intelligence. I put him out of his misery (or more likely into it) after thirty minutes of strained conversation.

"You wanna play?" I say in the sexy deep voice I use for such occasions.

He looks at me with his baby blues, pauses, sets down his ragged beer bottle, and nods. I leave to get the bedroom ready. Pull the drapes, put on the music, get out the poppers, and strategically place the condoms, latex gloves, and germicidal lubricant within easy reach. When I return, he's gulping down his third beer from the six-pack he brought, slightly panic-stricken.

I know by now that the only way to deal with straight men's inhibitions is to take charge right away. They need direction and don't really want to be given a choice.

"Come here," I demand in my deeper Daddy voice.

I lead him by the hand into the semidarkened bedroom.

"Stand here. Arms up," I bark like a drill instructor.

I make him face the wall and blindfold him. I reach under his clothes and slowly tease his body with my fingertips. When I get down to his cock, it's erect and strangely shaped. Long and large but twisting violently to the left.

I pull down his pants and Calvin Kleins and feel his small, firm ass, then slap it a couple times. He submits immediately. He likes being blindfolded. It's less embarrassing than having eye contact.

I order him to "Lie down on the bed. On your stomach!"

He reaches out blindly, finds the bed, and fumbles into position.

The rules have already been discussed and understood. He's my sex object, my slave boy, my compliant plaything.

I tie his hands and feet to the four corners of my bed with

leather restraints from the Pleasure Chest. I'd never let anyone tie me up on a first date, but this is the fantasy he had asked for when we talked before hitting the bedroom. He wanted a big, dominating Daddy, and I've always had those tendencies—even as a kid.

"I remember having dominant fantasies when I was as young as eight or nine," I said earlier, as we sat on the couch. "I had a blond, freckled, school friend who I thought was cute. I didn't think about having sex with him, but I had a daydream of holding him in a cabin in the woods as my prisoner. Sex never crossed my mind, but I thought it would be exciting to go to my cabin whenever I felt like it, and my captive would be there waiting for me."

"That's interesting," he replied, "cuz when I was about the same age, eight, I had this fantasy about being tied down, naked, on this table, and then people would come in and look at me. Not have sex with me, just look at me naked…and there was nothing I could do about it."

"So are you married? You have a girlfriend?" I asked.

He immediately tensed up. "I really don't want to talk about my personal life. Okay?"

"Okay. Have you ever done this before?"

"No. I never told anyone about my fantasy of being tied down naked, until now. I had forgotten it until you told me about yours."

When he cums, he cums softly—so softly that I'm not sure it's happened. Such control these straight men have.

As soon as I untie him, he pulls off the blindfold, and heads straight for the front door.

"You want coffee?" I ask. "You wanna sober up a bit before you drive?"

He doesn't. But he says, "Thank you" repeatedly like he

really means it—like I've done him a huge favor and he's deeply grateful.

"See you later," I say.

"Thank you!"

And with that he's out the door, rushing down the stairs so fast you'd think he was trying to outrun his subconscious—but disturbing thoughts are still snapping at his heels, like a pack of wolves with erections.

Straight men always freak out after coming in contact with the dick-hungry slut inside them. Their masculine clock just can't calculate who or what they are anymore. They get that tone in their voice that says, "Hey dude, I'm heterosexual. It never happened, and please don't call me again."

They lock their asshole up tight and throw away the key—until the next time they secretly desire dick, which in my experience is usually many months later. Don't ask me why. They need pussy daily, but cock can come once a mating season.

It's strange that I don't have a burning desire for a vagina two or three times a year. And if I did answer a straight sex ad and meet up with a married woman in the middle of the day and she fucked my brains out, I wouldn't be in deep denial, pretending it never happened. I'd be bragging to all my lesbian friends about how many orgasms she had.

MASTERING STEFAN

J. M. Snyder

Three years and Stefan's yet to find that certain someone who can take him to the precipice of lust, dangle him over the abyss, and shove him headlong into the darkness of his own desire. Someone who drives him to the edge but won't let him fall. Someone he can trust completely, body and soul, someone he can lose himself in. When a local gay bar called the Code hosts a fetish night, Stefan goes looking to be conquered.

August in Richmond is sweltering—even at quarter to midnight, the air is sticky like a wet rag and the humidity takes Stefan's breath away. He settles for a black latex vest, no undershirt, and a pair of bright blue latex boy-shorts so tight Daisy Duke would be jealous. The shorts make his buttocks look like two round rubber balls, high and tight, and the outline of his cock bulges along the top of his upper left thigh. The vest, tapering to twin points just above his narrow waist, only accentuates both assets.

But when he enters the bar, he's just one more body in the

crowded sea that undulates over the dance floor. Music pounds around him like the surf, washing him up to the bar with the rest of the driftwood. He orders a White Russian, his first mistake. Then he eases onto a vacant stool, his second. Just to wait for the drink, he reasons, but sitting at the bar in a place like this is social suicide. After his next Russian, Stefan stops trying to make eye contact with anyone other than the bartender. By his third, he thinks this party is a bust.

He stays, if only because the night is young and the drinks are cheap. Between refills he swivels around on the stool, leans back against the bar, and surveys the room around him. In the dim lighting, the bodies meld into one, a primordial animal that gyrates obscenely in time to the music as if masturbating to the beat. The thought turns Stefan on. He has to slide down a little to ease the chafe in his shorts—his dick tries to swell beneath the latex but the shorts won't give an inch, and the restriction only makes him harder. He shifts his package a bit, rearranges the goods, until the swollen tip of his cock ends dangerously close to the bottom hem of the shorts. As he presses against the stiff length, his eyes slip shut at the sweet ache that blossoms in him. *And no one to share it with*, he thinks.

As he turns back for his drink, a shadow detaches itself from the dance floor, heading his way. When Stefan spares a glance over one shoulder, the stranger takes that as an invitation and sidles up next to him at the bar. The guy is a few years older than Stefan, early forties at the most, with long blond hair tied back from his face with a thin leather strap at the nape of his neck. The arm closest to Stefan bulges with strength, the skin rough and ruddy from long exposure to the sun. Raising his glass, Stefan gives the stranger a drunken grin and has to shout over the crowd to be heard. "Hey."

A hand falls to Stefan's thigh, large fingers clamping down

on the erection that strains his shorts. Blunt fingertips trace the length and the latex warms beneath the touch. When the guy looks at him, Stefan's lower lip is caught between his teeth to bite back a half-muffled gasp that manages to escape anyway. The stranger has eyes like diamonds, so pale they're almost clear, rimmed with black kohl that gives him a deadly look, and the set of his jaw imbues him with a wrath worthy of any young god. "Please," Stefan sobs. He wants to give himself up to this man, with his white mesh tank top and his black rubber pants. The fingers on his dick make it hard to remember a time before their touch. Struggling not to appear too eager and failing miserably, Stefan wants to know, "Where?"

The guy doesn't answer. Far away in another world, the bartender sets another White Russian in front of Stefan, with a tall shot of amber whiskey to accompany it. The stranger knocks back the whiskey, never dropping his gaze from Stefan's. He holds Stefan prisoner in those crystal eyes, pins him to the stool like a captured moth. The hand on Stefan's thigh inches higher, the latex rolling up beneath it, until the tip of his dick dampens the stranger's palm. With one hand Stefan grabs on to the bar to hold himself steady; with the other, he dares to touch the stranger's muscled forearm and feels the tendons stand out beneath his fingers.

There at the bar, the guy sinks down to squat in front of Stefan's stool. Still silent, he turns Stefan to face him, spreading Stefan's legs until he's between them. His wide eyes watch Stefan closely, his thin, unsmiling lips not betraying any emotion while Stefan struggles to hold his back. He wants to throw himself at this man—he wants to be ravished, torn into from behind, latex stripped away as this stranger barrels inside. He feels his heart beating where the boy-shorts cut into his upper thighs and wants to beg this stranger to take him now. But more than that, he wants to be taken without having to ask.

Slowly, the guy rolls back the hem of Stefan's shorts—just the leg where his dick pulses. He peels the latex an inch or two away from Stefan's cockhead; the shorts are too tight to allow anything more. Some part of Stefan's mind whispers that his dick is out in front of a couple of hundred people, what the hell's he doing here? But the mere fact that he's exposed in a bar and the night doesn't come to a screeching halt around him is enough to make his dick begin to weep. At the first drop of jism, the stranger leans closer, his hair tickling Stefan's thighs, *closer*, until his hot whiskey-wet lips kiss the tip of Stefan's dick.

"Oh, god," he moans. His fingers dig into the guy's arm, claw at the bar. His hips rise up off the stool, but his trembling legs are too weak to hold his own weight and he plops back down. The latex cuts across his erection like a tourniquet, igniting a dull fire in his balls that smolders with lust. A soft tongue rubs across the spongy glans of his cock, tickling him, teasing. Saliva and cum slick the latex around the head of his shaft and the stranger's hand presses down on Stefan's still-sheathed length, kneading him through the shorts, working him toward release. When that mouth closes over his bulbous tip, the stranger tongues a tender spot just below his slit and sucks until Stefan comes with an explosive orgasm that threatens to rip him asunder.

Stefan bucks up off the stool, his hand knocking aside the untouched Russian waiting for him, and white liqueur splatters the bar like the load he shoots into the stranger's willing throat. As the other man stands, Stefan sighs, "Please." His hand trails down the guy's arm, catches for a moment in those strong fingers, then falls to his lap, spent. *Take me home*, he wants to say, his mind filled with images of the two of them entwined together in someone's bed, but he can't seem to remember how to put those thoughts into words so he just murmurs again, "Please."

The stranger pulls something from his back pocket—a business card. Tenderly he lifts Stefan's now-limp member and slides the card into the sticky wetness between Stefan's cock and thigh. Then he rolls the latex down again to cover the too-tender tip of Stefan's dick. The paper feels like cardboard shoved into his shorts.

Then the guy fades back into the crowd. No words, not even a name. Stefan reaches for the White Russian, needing a drink, only to find ice cubes melting on the bar.

It takes him half a week to work up the courage to call the number on the card. He dials it from work, waiting until the office empties out at lunchtime to pick up the phone. The first try, he hits a six instead of a two and has to start again. The second try rings once, twice, three times before Stefan thinks he hears someone in another cubicle and lets the phone slip back into the cradle. He stands, stretches, looks around but he's just hearing things—he's alone. This time he dials quickly before he can lose his nerve, but someone answers on the first ring and startles him speechless. "What is it?" a gruff voice asks. If Stefan had to give a sound to the nameless stranger from the Code, this would be it.

Beneath his desk, Stefan shuffles his feet together like a nervous teenager. "Um, hi," he starts, then remembers he's at work and lowers his voice. He glances at the business card again but only sees the number he's dialed and the word MASTER beneath it. The fact that it's spelled out in black and white stirs his blood. Unsure of how to begin, Stefan admits, "I got your card."

"Did I give it to you?" the voice wants to know. *Master*, Stefan thinks, mouthing the word to try it on for size. "Or did someone else pass it along? Because I'm very select in who I give this number to and if you didn't get it from me, hang up."

"No," Stefan hurries to explain, "I got it from you. At least I think so. Saturday night, at the Code?" His words are met with a stony silence so loud, it hurts Stefan's ears. "I was at the bar. Getting a drink? And you...I don't know, you came up to me and just sort of..."

He trails off. "Sort of what?" Master prompts.

Stefan lowers his voice. "I had on these shorts. Made out of latex?"

"Are you asking or telling me?" Master wants to know.

"Blue shorts." Stefan remembers how he had to peel them off when he got home, digging the latex out of his ass after that blow job. "You rolled back the leg and then..." His face feels hot and he has to rub his hands down the front of his slacks to dry his sweaty palms. "You...you—"

Master demands, "Say it."

"I'm at work," Stefan whispers. More silence, and beads of sweat break out along the back of his neck just below his hairline. With a furtive look around at the empty office, Stefan whispers, "You sucked me off. Remember?" It's almost a plea.

But warmth floods the voice on the other end of the line, and Stefan sighs with relief. "Ah, yes. You. I wondered when you'd call."

"Really?" A silly grin tugs at Stefan's lips but he twists his mouth into a frown to tamp it down. Hoping he sounds suave and nonchalant despite the pounding of his heart, he shrugs and asks, "So, you busy tonight? Or something?"

He expects a coy answer along the lines of, *What do you have in mind?* But Master cuts to the chase. "Tell me what you're wearing."

"Now?" Stefan asks, surprised. "I'm at work."

"If I drop by this evening," Master clarifies, "what'll you have on? Better yet, what will I have to take *off* to get to that sweet candy ass of yours?"

"I'm...I—" Stefan stutters, searching for something to say. What on earth will he wear? Anything Master wants, anything at all. Did he honestly say he's coming over tonight? *Oh, god.* Lamely, he whispers, "I don't know."

"Shit." For a moment Stefan thinks he's angry at him, but before he can stumble through an apology Master says, "What's your fetish? Leather, Saran Wrap, what?"

Stefan mumbles, "Latex." He likes the smooth feel of the thin plastic—wet, slick, and molded to his body, or hot against his sweaty skin, unyielding as he strains against it. He likes wetsuits and galoshes and latex gloves that snap into place, the way they feel rubbing along his flesh, the way they smell pressed to his nose. Once he masturbated in the dressing room of a department store while wearing nothing but a raincoat so new, it squeaked every time he moved. Scuba magazines are porn to him—pictures of men in formfitting suits that he imagines ripping apart to get at the tender meat inside. He dreams of running in the rain wearing nothing but a slicker, a cold rush of air breezing against his balls as someone unseen chases him. It's a familiar dream, one he's had since middle school, and though he's never been caught, he knows that whoever hunts him down wants to pin him down and fuck him right there in the mud and the rain. He can almost picture the slicker rucked up over his ass and knows just what the rain would feel like streaming down his pale skin. Whenever he has that dream he wakes up so hard, it only takes one or two good jerks to get him off.

In his ear, Master murmurs, "Latex." The word sounds like a promise in his voice. Before Stefan can reply, Master continues, "This is what I want. You'll be home by what, six?"

"Yes," Stefan says. His voice cracks and he clears his throat to try again. "Six, yes, I'll be there."

"Leave your door unlocked," Master commands, "and put on something—you have a full bodysuit, right?"

Stefan has two, both black latex. One has zippers strategically placed for easy access, which he has yet to put to use. The other has seen more wear—he's modified it himself, adding a rubber cock sheath that juts from the front like a handle and a tiny ball sewn into the butt to press between his buttocks. That's his solo suit, the one he puts on when it's just him and his hand, and unfortunately that's all too often. He likes to put it on and sit in the bathtub, the shower pounding down around him as he massages his cock through the sheath and grinds his hips back against the spigot to work that little ball around and around his asshole. "I have things to wear," he admits.

"Get dressed, then," Master tells him, "with me in mind. This is the important part now—you can't get off before I get there, you hear me? Sit on your hands if you have to but keep them out of your ass and away from your cock. You understand?"

"Yes," Stefan breathes. "Yes, Sir."

"What's my card say?" Master prompts.

Stefan raises the business card to his nose and can still smell his own spunk lingering on the paper. "Yes, *Master*."

Per Master's instructions, Stefan doesn't lock the front door to his townhouse when he comes home from work. His is a quiet neighborhood, no one will enter, but it turns him on to strip down to his underwear in the foyer knowing that someone could walk in on him. Kicking his clothes aside, he takes the steps two at a time to the bedroom, where he peels off his underwear and snags the zippered latex suit from his closet. He's hard already just thinking about wearing it, but he wants to prolong the anticipation, do things right. He goes into the bathroom then, where he leaves the door open just in case Master comes in and hears the shower running. Stefan takes his time, lathering his cock and balls and ass, slipping one finger inside himself and gasping at the sting of soap on hidden flesh. By the time he cuts off the water, his dick is tender to the touch but he promised he wouldn't get off until Master arrives and it's all he can do to hold back. He empties half a bottle of baby oil into his palms, rubs it over his nipples and chest, down his belly, slathering his erection and balls and the trembling skin between his legs. There's a cock ring he keeps stretched around a hairbrush; he rolls it off and slides it down into place against the base of his shaft, to help him stay hard without blowing his wad. He applies more baby oil to his buttocks, lifting and spreading them apart to coat the cleft between them, then he steps into the suit and begins to zip it into place.

The suit fits like a second skin. A long zipper runs from the waist to the raised collar, which Stefan tugs up with relish, enjoying the slow tightening of latex around his body. He smoothes his hands down his chest, savors his own touch through the plastic, cups his throbbing cock and works the latex against his balls. The material glides along his skin easily, frictionless from the baby oil. The tab of a small zipper dangles between Stefan's legs and he thumbs it open an inch or two, just enough to slip inside and strum his perineum. Grabbing the edge of the sink, he squats a little to finger himself and wonders when Master will arrive.

Master. Reluctantly Stefan zips the suit shut. His hands shake as he washes them in the sink, his entire body humming with the pleasure that radiates from his crotch. He won't come now, he won't give in, not yet. Not alone. He heads downstairs then, where he'll try to think of something other than the stretch and pull of latex across his skin. But each footstep is a spark that ignites his blood, each movement cranks his lust up another notch. He barely makes it down the stairs, gasping as he descends, grabbing at the rail to keep from passing out from sheer ecstasy. At the foot of the stairs he has to catch his breath, the suit is so *tight*, it pinches him in all the right places, and his whole body *aches* with the need for release. Somehow he makes it across the living room to the couch. His hands are drawn to the bulge at the front of his suit as if magnetized— he can't stop touching himself. Again and again he brings himself to the brink of orgasm, but each time he manages to bite it back, hold it in.

Wait for Master, he tells himself. It takes all the strength he has to keep that thought foremost in his mind. *It'll be better together, don't do it alone, he said not to come, he said to wait...* Somehow, incredibly, Stefan forces himself to wait.

Minutes pass, each one an eternity. Stefan sits on his hands as Master told him to, palms down to keep from rubbing his fingers along the crack of his ass. He watches the clock on his VCR and the green numbers blink at him like staring cats. Seven o'clock comes and goes, eight running to catch up behind it, nine looming on the horizon like a death sentence. By nine-thirty every part of him beats in time with his heart. How much longer? Another moment more and he'll explode.

When the telephone rings in the kitchen, Stefan feels the front of his latex suit dampen with a quick spurt of precum. "Shit!" That was *too* close. *Let it ring*, he thinks as one hand absently begins to rub at his crotch, but after several minutes of the insistent noise, a thought occurs to him. *Master*. Launching himself off the couch, Stefan staggers into the kitchen and answers the phone with a breathless, "Yes?"

In his ear, Master purrs, "Did I set you off?"

"Almost," Stefan admits. He leans back against the wall, sated just hearing his Master's rough voice. "Where are you?"

Master counters the question with one of his own. "What if I said I can't make it tonight?"

Discouragement floods Stefan—he wants arms around him, kisses across his brow, someone else's fingers in him for once. Is that asking too much? "Why not?" he asks. It sounds like an accusation but he doesn't care. "I'm waiting—"

"Good boy," Master says.

"What?" Stefan asks, confused. Then it hits him and he has to ask, "Is this some sort of game to you?" The thought angers him—what if this guy is laughing right now because he got Stefan so worked up just waiting for him to show? "Don't fuck with me, *Master*."

A lengthy silence stretches between them and Stefan fights the urge to apologize. He listens to Master's breath, tries to imagine what might be going on behind those crystal clear eyes. It seems like forever before Master finally speaks. "This is not a game," he says, and Stefan believes him. "It's a test. I've met lots of guys who say whatever they think I want them to say just to get fucked, and that's not what I'm looking for here. I want someone to spoil, Stefan. I want someone to worship, someone to protect. I want someone who wants *me*, who wants every *part* of me. Someone who trusts me enough to know that I will never, ever let them go. That sort of relationship isn't easy to come by."

"I know," Stefan whispers. Doesn't he want those things too? He wants to be spoiled, worshipped, protected. *I want that someone you're talking about to be me.*

"So this is a test," Master says again. "I want to see how far you'll go for me, how long you'll wait. I might not show up today, or tomorrow, or two weeks from now. But if you're as serious as I am about this, then you'll be ready whenever I come for you. Can you do that, Stefan? Can you wait for me?"

Stefan doesn't know. He chokes back tears that clog his throat and whimpers, "I'm so *close*."

Master tells him, "Wait for me. If you pass the test, Stefan, I promise to make every single one of your dreams come true. But if you fail..."

He trails off and lets Stefan imagine what failure will bring. Another long moment passes, then Master whispers in Stefan's ear, "Don't fail me, boy. I want you."

Stefan leans back against the wall as the phone slips from his nerveless fingers. When he starts to slide down to retrieve it, the latex suit squeezes against his erection with a sweet pain that pounds through him like a toothache and he doesn't dare squat down any farther just in case he comes all over the place. Pushing away from the wall, he glares at the clock on the wall above the kitchen sink and replays their conversation in his head. Did Master honestly say it'd be two weeks? Dear god, Stefan will die before then. He can picture it already: dead at thirty-two, found wrapped in plastic with a smile on his face and a hard-on to make *rigor mortis* look limp. Beneath his breath, Stefan mutters, "Two weeks, my ass. I can't wait that long."

Behind him, a familiar voice growls in his ear, "Me either."

Stefan starts to turn but a black hood descends over his head, blinding him. "Master?" he asks, hands fluttering to his neck as the hood tightens beneath his chin. It cuts off all sensation—he can't see, can't hear, can barely *breathe*, and the sudden rush this gives him is like a jolt of adrenaline to his heart. Strong hands grab his wrists and pin them behind his back. Very faintly, Stefan hears the metallic click of handcuffs closing into place and an experimental tug proves that his arms are secured. "Thank you," he sighs. "Master, thank you. I didn't think—"

Master interrupts him. "Two rules." He speaks close to Stefan's ear to be heard through the hood, his breath hot through the material. Latex, Stefan would recognize this heady vinyl smell anywhere. "One, don't fight the cuffs. They tighten the more you struggle and I want this to be fun."

Stefan nods. "Two," Master continues, stepping around Stefan to face him, "I'm not gagging you for a reason. This is fun for us both, you hear me? And you might be the one trussed up but you call the shots. One word—any word, even if it's my name, or God's, or holy fuck *yes*—and I stop. One word and this all ends. I walk out, it's over. You got that?"

Again, Stefan nods. Beneath the mask, he clamps his lips tight together. No words. He wants this, he *needs* it, he'll never talk again if he has to. *Just please*, he thinks as the first drop of sweat trickles down his brow. His hands itch to wipe it away but he doesn't dare move a muscle. *Please.*

Trailing a finger down the front of Stefan's suit, Master traces the zipper with one short nail. Lower, his finger outlines Stefan's cock, then finds the small zipper that closes off his crotch. "What do we have here?" he asks. From the sound of his voice, he's kneeling in front of Stefan now, *god*. When he plucks at the zipper behind Stefan's balls, teasing him, Stefan moans but doesn't speak. He won't say a word. He *won't*.

That zipper opens slowly, one notch at a time, an excruciating wait. Wisps of cool air sneak beneath the latex to soothe his fevered skin. Another notch, two, and his testicles slip free from the suit. Then the zipper opens a little wider and his tortured cock finally *finally* escapes the tight confines of its prison. "Hello again," Master says, playful. He runs his thumb along the bottom of Stefan's shaft from base to tip and kisses the damp head. Stefan bites his lower lip until he can taste the coppery tinge of blood. His control is slipping, he feels it loosening with the dribble of precum he can't hold back. Master licks it away. "Not yet. I'll tell you when." His hand eases between Stefan's legs to rub at his latex-sheathed buttocks. "I want in there," he tells Stefan, tapping against the taut material that separates his finger from Stefan's quivering hole. "What do you think? Can I come in?"

Stefan clamps his mouth shut, he won't be tricked, but he gives Master a vigorous nod to show that he wants to let him in. Still, it takes years for Master to stop fondling him and stand. His hands smooth up Stefan's hips and around his waist, and when they find Stefan's bound hands, his fingers lace through Stefan's as Master pulls him into a tight embrace. That hot breath again, matching Stefan's own; this time it flutters along the face of the hood, tickles the small holes that allow Stefan to breathe, the smell of sex on it like a breath mint. Master presses his mouth to Stefan's and tongues the latex keeping them apart with an urgency that makes Stefan's knees buckle. In a harsh whisper, Master asks, "How badly do you want me?"

A wordless cry of frustration tears from Stefan's throat and Master laughs. "This is a test," he reminds Stefan, releasing him. One hand trails along Stefan's shoulder as Master circles to stand behind him. "Remember that. You're doing well. Good boy."

Master pets Stefan's back then moves lower, rubs down between his asscheeks and up again, tantalizing. When he dips along Stefan's crack a second time, his other hand presses against the small of Stefan's back, leaning him forward. Stefan complies, his ass now sitting in Master's firm palm. A thick thumb follows the curve of his butt, feeling through the latex for an entrance, and to himself, Master mutters, "How the hell am I supposed to get in here?"

Stefan has a few ideas, but he doesn't offer them. With a displeased grunt, Master moves away to rummage through one of the kitchen drawers and Stefan almost stumbles from the sudden lack of support. "Where do you keep the knives?"

Master wants to know. Beneath the hood, Stefan closes his eyes and takes a deep, shuddery breath. So many questions...*testing me*, Stefan reminds himself. He hears Master opening drawers, cursing when he can't find what he's looking for. *You're here for me*, Stefan wants to say. *Tear through the suit with your teeth if you have to, just get back to me.*

"Aha." A drawer closes and Stefan waits to be touched. When Master returns, though, he grabs Stefan's upper arm in a stern fist and pulls him along to another spot in the kitchen. Stefan follows, obedient—what else can he do? He loves this attention, the details, the thought behind each movement. The latex binds him into his own inner world where Master looms as the only reality. His hands are all Stefan can feel; his voice, all Stefan hears. Without sight, his other senses have taken over and he can even sense Master breathing, as if they're both part of the same beast.

When Master stops, Stefan bumps into him. "Down," Master commands, the strong hand against Stefan's back forcing him to bend at the waist until he finds himself facedown on the kitchen table. Booted feet kick his legs apart, spreading them wide. Master rubs at his ass, seeking entry. "Let me at this apple bottom of yours," he says, stroking between Stefan's legs. Once or twice the tips of his fingers brush Stefan's balls and he gasps. *Now*, he thinks, the word a litany in his mind. *Now, take me now, Jesus Master, now!* If only he could beg out loud...

Finding a spot he likes, Master pinches the latex and pulls it away from Stefan's skin. "Hold still," he cautions. Stefan hears the *snip snip* of scissors and catches his breath, his mind a whirl of white panic. *What*— "Trust me."

The scissors pierce the latex easily. For the briefest moment Stefan feels a cold blade of steel on his heated flesh, then the latex tears enough for Master to throw the scissors aside and work at the material with his hands. The latex splits a bit more, gaping above Stefan's puckered hole. "There you are," Master says with a laugh. Stefan laughs too, but the sound dissolves into a sharp intake of breath when Master's hot tongue licks beneath the latex to taste him. His legs slide wider apart, he sinks into the table, his entire body numbs from desire and lust, and his cock stands tall as Master rims him. "So tender," he sighs, the words kissed into Stefan's buttocks. His tongue delves under the latex to touch the base of Stefan's sac and saliva trickles down in its wake. Soft, maddening, Master's tongue swabs Stefan's ass, wetting him, readying him.

Then he stands, his touch gone, and Stefan sobs with need. "Puh—" he starts, *please*, but he catches himself in time and bites back the rest. *Please*. He hears a belt buckle hit the floor and a second later, the cool tip of a huge cock pokes his ass. His sphincter contracts, his muscles work to draw Master in, but he's no longer in charge here. Master holds off, probably enjoying the sight of a half-hidden ass flexing beneath his dick, who knows? Time stops, folds in on itself, turns back, and Stefan's crying now, hot tears burn the hood that blinds him, *please*. When one finger finally eases inside him, he lets out an angry scream like a spoiled child. *NOW!*

Finally Master eases his thick cock into Stefan. "Shh," he murmurs, rubbing Stefan's back with one hand as he glides inside. His other hand finds Stefan's dick and blunt fingers roll off the cock ring that holds him back. "There you go. How's that feel?" Released, *Thank you*, Stefan mouths silently. He thrusts into Master's fist, finding a rhythm that matches Master's own slow fuck. He's earth-shattering, this man—he drives into Stefan all the way to the base of his shaft, holds the position a moment or two, long enough to send bursts of pleasure shattering through Stefan like a million shards of glass, then pulls out until the head of his cock almost slips free. In again, harder, the wait a little longer, then the mind-bending slow draw back out. In, out, a steady pace. Stefan comes immediately, slicking Master's hand with his juices, and lets himself be coaxed to a second climax. He gasps with each entry, sucking in the latex that covers his mouth until the inside of the hood is slick with sweat and spit, and it presses against his face with a hot dampness. He moans with desire, his throat thick with lust, but he doesn't dare say a word because he never, ever wants this to end.

Sometime later, Master loosens the hood and pulls it up over the bridge of Stefan's nose. Fresh air floods his senses, stunning him. Then warm lips cover his in a tender kiss. "You can speak now," Master murmurs against his mouth. "You passed the test."

Stefan gulps in Master's breath. It takes a second or two for him to find something, *anything*, to say. When he can, he asks, "What's that mean?"

"You're mine."

Another kiss, just as loving as the first. Master licks Stefan's lips before parting them, seeking his tongue. Stefan pours everything he has into the kiss, the only touch he feels—everything from his waist down is overstimulated and buzzes with a faint numbness. Even his shoulders have lost all sensation, and he no longer feels the handcuffs on his wrists. His fingers could have fallen off for all he knows. Never has he felt this hollow, this empty, this *used*. Like a well-worn tool, or a favorite toy. Master rubs the back of his neck, kisses him hungrily, whispers that he's been a good boy, he's done well. Stefan melts beneath the touch.

When the hood finally comes all the way off, Stefan has to blink back the stark light that blinds him. Both hands on the clock on the wall point at the twelve but that means nothing to him. Midnight, noon? He doesn't know, doesn't care. Master helps him stand, then turns Stefan around to face him. Disappointment stabs through him when he notices Master is fully dressed in a long-sleeved black latex shirt and pants so tight, they look painted on. If his ass didn't throb from Master's earlier ministrations, Stefan could almost believe the man just arrived. In a petulant voice, he asks, "You're going?"

"I don't want to," Master concedes. His long blond hair is tied at his nape, just the way Stefan remembers it, and even in the bright kitchen light, his eyes are as clear as glass. Picking at the zipper pull under Stefan's chin, Master asks, "Can you handle more?" Stefan nods quickly, yes. Fuck the hour, and fuck work tomorrow, as long as this man fucks him again, and again, and again. A small smile curves Master's thin lips. "How about a little game?"

"Sure," Stefan agrees, eager to please.

Master's hand drifts down Stefan's chest, his gaze following. "There's only one key to those cuffs," Master tells him. "I have it on me. Somewhere. To play the game, you must undress me first, then probe around until you find it." Stefan grins as Master adds, "Using only your mouth, your tongue, and your teeth."

Stefan's abused cock jerks to attention at the promise of a long night ahead. He can't wait to find out what he wins when he finds the key.

MARKING TERRITORY

Sean Meriwether

The stench of ripe piss, like rotted fruit, penetrates through your hangover and swells with your growing consciousness. Your hands are bound behind you, tight, and your elevated ass is shoved against the metal cover that walls you in. The dark world beats you down and you plead to black out and erase the time.

A muted red light enflames your tight enclosure and you are tossed forward across the cheap carpet. The only thing you have on, besides the skivvies that you were wearing in your girlfriend's bed, is a sticky sheen of urine that glows red across your pale skin. You are paralyzed when you hear a car door open and footsteps moving closer; you shut your eyes, hold your breath, and hope they think you're dead. Your mind reels with explanations and skirts the truth as skillfully as a junkie rationalizes his next hit.

Two voices approach, men you recognize with a chill. The Southern cadence of Red's voice, the con-man who'd gotten you into this mess, and the deep rumble of Vix44, the biggest motherfucker you've ever seen. The pair belong to Havana, the man who'd been stupid enough to trust you with ten kilos of Columbian, and his thugs are about to make an example out of you; don't cross Havana.

The trunk rises and you are blinded by sharp daylight. Red pops a cherry into his mouth, bites down hard, spits the pit out into your face. "Awake, shitbag?" He smiles, his mustache riding up under his thin nose. This was the same guy who'd taken you to Havana a year ago claiming you'd make a mint, a fuckin' pile of dough. "Old man's gonna skin you alive, asshole," he says now. Red unzips his fly and sends a fragrant thick stream into your upturned face. You turn away as your eyes and mouth are invaded by his salty piss. "Baste that piglet," his partner says. Old Vix44. They said his name came from the dimensions of his cock—four by four—and having seen the size of his hands, you'd believe it.

Vix steps up to the trunk and smiles down at your pathetic figure. "Gonna marinate the pork," he snorts and pulls out his hose to wash you down. Before he shoots his squirt, he makes sure you get a full eye of the weapon he's got in his hand. Even soft it looks like the arm and fist of a child, and he nods his head and pisses on you as the reality sinks in. You'd rather be shot than split open by that thing. "Have me a pork chop on a plate. You bacon, boy?"

Beyond Vix44 you can see blue sky and trees, fresh air, and they seem as unreal as your plans for escape. Vix drops a gob of spit down on your head and slams the trunk closed, trapping you in the stink of their fresh piss. You wonder how long you've been stuck there, an unwilling toilet, and how much longer they could drive around before they put a slug in your head and dump you on the street, an advertisement of Havana's power.

The car bumps along rutted roads, your body tossed around

like a cheap slag, making your empty stomach hitch. You'd die to pass out again as the car swerves to hit an eternal series of potholes and ditches. The bruises on your arms and legs paint your skin darker shades of blue and purple.

When the car finally stops, your body still feels the movement, like sea legs. It seems as if hours pass before the trunk opens and the oil-tainted air rushes inside. Red smiles down into your squinting eyes. "Had enough, piss-ass? Man, you so disappoint." He looks like a ferret in a suit as he plucks a cherry from his pocket and sucks it into his mouth. "Get him outta there, Vix. Havana wants this skinny shit."

Vix44 lowers his powerful arms and picks you up in a bear hug. You choke on his thick cologne. The bristles of his beard scratch against your face. "He is a pretty thing, isn't he, Red? Pretty little girly-boy." He drops you on the concrete of the garage floor and you look up at your own car, the brand new BMW that you bought with the money scammed off Havana. *Stupid shit,* you say to yourself. *How was I so stupid?*

"You ever been to a pig roast, boy?" Vix44 asks you.

You shake your head sadly. "No, sir. I ain't no pig today. Come on, Vix, let us go and you can keep the car. I'll leave, I swear it, go where nobody knows me."

Vix44 laughs in your ear as he forces you up on your feet and holds you against him. "You're my piglet, boy." His groin presses into your cuffed hands and you think about squeezing down on his package. Vix backs up a step and slaps the side of your head. "Don't be a fool bastard, pork chop. You'll get more of that than you want."

Red complains about the smell of you, but it doesn't bother Vix44; he hauls you through a door by the back of your underpants, your cock and balls pulled up into the tight sack created by your betraying briefs. He tosses you onto the cement slab floor of a paneled room and steps away. You stare at the reflective black shoes of Havana's feet, whose first comment is a kick in the head.

"You little scumbag shit," he says, his husky voice dropping an octave below normal. "You think you can cut me out, huh? You think you're such a smart prick that you can scam me? Do you know who you are messing with, or do I gotta remind you that you're playing with big boys, here?" He drops his cigar next to your face, grinds it out with his shoe, and plants the hot sole of his foot against your face. "I warned you when Red brought you in, you do what I tell you, when I tell you. You don't think for yourself, got it? I want some sign that you get me, shit for brains." He squats down next to you. "Geez, you smell like fuckin' hell. Vix, man, you're one crazy fuck." Havana laughs, then after an uncomfortable interval, Vix44 and Red join in.

You apologize, and apologize, and apologize; a whine of *sorry*s that you ever were stupid enough to try to one-up Havana. "Gonna teach you a lesson, kid. Next time you sit down on your brains, you're gonna think of me, you got it?"

Vix44 hauls you up by the seat of your drawers and slips them down around your knees. He pushes you over to a counter and you brace your shoulders against it. "You owe me fifty grand, kid. I want it. All of it. You got twenty-four hours." Havana lights another cigar, and the earthy smoke fills your lungs. "All right, Vix, rip him up." The room grows achingly quiet as the boss turns and leaves. You can hear his footsteps groan up the stairs and across the floorboards. A football game comes on, loud enough to drown out any noise you might make.

Vix44 unzips his pants and steps out of them. You can see his socks close in on you from between your parted legs. "Come on, man, I get it. I learned my lesson. You don't gotta...Shit, Vix.

This isn't fair." You close your eyes so that you won't cry and hope it will be over quick.

"Basted pork, you gotta love it." Vix44 spits on his latexed dick and shoves it up into your ass until all you see is black and stars. You can feel the burn of his rod, and you pray that you'll be able to walk or shit again. Vix burrows into you, holds you by the waist and pumps you full of flesh. "Yeah, piglet, ride me." His cock pummels you, spreading your asscheeks wide open. Vix44 grunts as he fucks you, holds you like he's jerking himself off with your body, and you feel him in your guts, your lungs, your throat.

His sweating arms hold you down as he pulls out and a cold breeze blows up into the gaping hole he leaves behind. You wish he'd put it back in before your guts spill out between your legs. He slaps your tender ass and the shocking pain sends a chill over your skin and your face tingles.

"Let's go, Vix. Plug the guy and get it over with." Red pops a cherry in his mouth and sucks it into his cheek.

"Gonna enjoy myself a little first with this piglet here." Vix44 forces you down on your knees, and you are confronted with the shit-spattered rubber on his cock. "Give me some blow, piggie, blow your daddy." He peels the condom off and drops it with a plop at your knees and steps up to you, his cock smelling like your ass. He forces the tip in between your lips and you gag as the salty meat slides deep into your mouth, filling the back of your throat. He eases out, gently, then rams it back in, filling your head. Your mouth is in shock and salvia builds up and spills out, running along the shaft of Vix's cock and dribbling over his hairy balls. "That's the worst head I've ever had, gonna fuck you raw," Vix warns and you make an effort to sweeten the deal and get him off so he won't have to fuck you again. "That's better, piggie, yeah." He rides your head.

Swallowing his meat brings tears to your eyes, but as he pumps your face, you catch his rhythm and bob your head timed by his thrusts, tasting the silvery precum as it flows into your mouth. "Aw' right. Kid's got it down. Gonna turn you into a first rate cocksucker, cheese dick...yeah. Oh fuck." Vix pulls out and jerks his dick into your face, and you are bathed in a shower of cum as he jets onto your chin, chest, and legs. He hovers until a thin stream of piss follows and trickles over your head. "You gotta give this one here a go, Red. Kid was rough at first, but he's a natural. Got him all warmed up for ya."

Red spits the cherry out into his palm, stares at it, then shakes his head. "Your job, Vix, not mine. Let's go, get the kid, dump him in the car. Get him outta here before Mrs. H. gets home." He drops the cherry back into his mouth and then spits the pit on the floor near your knees.

"You don't gotta do it, man. I don't wanna die."

"Havana says you get to go, little fish. You tell your smokin' buddies who's in charge here, and you tell them what will happen if they try to fuck over Havana, you got that? You're the example. They're fish food." To finalize his point, Red takes his squirt on you with his semi-erect cock.

Vix44 zips up and then picks you up by your handcuffed wrists and drags you back to the car. "Have half a mind to keep this pussy right where I can find him. Tightest ass I've ever had."

"Havana says to dump him. You listenin', kid? You don't do your job you're gonna spend the rest of your life eatin' his spunk, got it?"

You nod your head frantically. "Yeah, Red, I hear you." Your jaw is stiff, your ass like burning fire.

Vix44 lowers you back into your own trunk, and you think the next car will have a bigger one. You collapse against the blue carpet, smelling of piss and spunk and feeling wide at both ends.

Red spits a cherry pit on you before he closes you in. They back out the car and careen through the streets, tossing you around in the bruised dark.

When the car finally stops it is nighttime. You can hear the chatter and gibber of your block, music blasting from Skeeter's car, Elmo and his girl shouting. Vix44 lifts you out and drops you in the gutter but not before poking a thumb in your wounded asshole.

"You learn your lesson, boy, and you better teach it too or Vix and I'll be back for you," Red says. The two men smile and nod at each other. "We'll be back tomorrow for the fifty grand you owe Havana. Better have it. Six o'clock."

Vix44 smiles widely. "Don't make us wait, bacon. You don't wanna piss me off." He uncuffs one wrist and drags you over to the bus sign and clamps the open side to it. "Tell your tale, pork chop." The men get back into your car and drive down the block, leaving you naked, stained, and bleeding and bound where you stand. The guys from the street start to gather around you. Your boys who you used to trust, who sold with you, sold for you, now poking and laughing at your skinny frame.

"Oh, shit, Vix44 done that boy good." Skeeter laughs and his girl, Tamara, squeals with derisive laughter. "Won't even need to sit down to shit," Elmo says. More catcalls and whistles as you struggle to squeeze out of the handcuffs, and when Jimmie comes to your rescue with the bolt-cutters, you are already planning your escape. "Havana gonna get you, boy," Skeeter says as you crawl up the fire escape to your apartment window, "Havana's gonna blow your mind."

A CERTAIN UNDERSTANDING

Ethan Thomas

You stretch the scarf tight between your fists. Heat rushes to my face, but I stare straight through you, unblinking. It's that or meet your eyes. You jerk your hands apart, daring me to look, and the faint pulse in my groin echoes the snap of the fabric a beat later. From the quirk in your voice, you haven't missed the tightness of my jeans.

"Is this what you want?"

"Whatever." I shrug and suck smoke between my teeth. "Always thought silk was pussy, myself."

You pluck the cigarette from my lips, flick it away. It dies on the hotel's pockmarked floorboards. I frown—the cig could have been useful—and then my chin is pinched hard between your thumb and forefinger, captured. Your breath stirs my lashes, hotter than the cherry on my smoke ever could have been. You squeeze tighter, and I grin. This might work out after all.

"On my knees or my back?" My gaze drifts sideways, away from you.

Your nails dig into my cheeks. "Look at me."

I don't have to. I've already looked once, seen everything I need to know: beach-boy hair, tanned skin, muscles that speak of exercise and aggression. I fight just a little, urging you to put some meat behind your grip. You have everything I need, if only you'd use it.

"Look at me."

Another glance, nothing more, and your smile fills my vision. The curve of your lips is even softer than your pretty scarf. Without warning, a single rivulet of cold sweat glides down my bare back. My nipples stiffen. I step away, expecting a struggle, but you let me go. My flesh goose-pimples.

"Back or knees?" I repeat. Even to my own ears, my voice sounds small and strained.

You dip your head, close the distance between us again. All I can smell is candy. Your mouth ghosts over mine. "Whatever you like."

My lip curls. This isn't what you promised. Your own jeans already hang open, exposing a small thatch of blond hair. I make a show of kicking off my own denims and throw them in your face. You don't move. Angry now, I flop back on the naked mattress and spread my legs. My cock lies limp against my thigh, just like every other time we've been together.

Moments pass. I glare at the ceiling, count the water spots. "Do you have the balls for this or not?"

"Do you?"

In response I lift my arms above my head and rattle the headboard.

"Good." You trail the silk lightly over my abdomen before looping it once around my wrists, securing me loosely to the rusted bars. "Too tight?"

I don't bother laughing. Your broad hands find my hips, but I don't look down.

"You could pull free," you continue, "but you won't. You're exactly where you want to be."

My shoulders tense. Your fingers linger on my thighs, tracing old scars better not explained. Your touch might be feathers on my skin. My breath jerks in my chest.

"I have to tie you up, is that it? Force pleasure on you?" Gentle now, you grasp my chin again. Slowly my gaze drifts from the cracked stucco overhead. Your smile stays tender as you descend. Throat, nipples, and navel—you taste them all, each graze of your lips somehow more horrible than any slap or burn could be. Each time I gasp, trying to squirm from beneath you, but you shove me down. That's so close, that's almost what I need, but now your head is between my legs, my cock in the warm hollow of your cheek. You bob as if you have all the time in the world, looking up at me from beneath the tangle of your hair.

I swallow. "Don't—"

You press slick lips against mine, cutting me off. A string of spit stretches between us as you pull back. You gather it with your fingers and reach between my legs. It won't be enough. Suddenly I have air again. I wrench my knees apart, daring you to push. You lean forward, grope beneath the mattress, and pull out a small tube of lubricant. The sight of it is almost more than I can bear. Very nearly I tell you to stop, that I cannot endure this, but then your finger is inside me, careful and wet. After forever, a second digit slides deep, stroking that spot high inside me. When you finally push your cock inside, it is with one smooth, painless thrust.

I make a strangled sound in my throat, as if I am gagged as well as bound, but it isn't enough for you.

"Tell me what you want," you whisper, pumping in and out

of my ass so slowly that tears run down my cheeks.

Somehow, miraculously, the scarf is still tied. I grab it with both hands, twist it tighter about my wrists. An instant later, your arms slide around me, and I rock my hips hard. Yeah, this will be all right. *Grab* me, *fuck* me—

Your head comes to rest on my chest, and I sob.

Breath shudders against my collarbone. "Please," you whisper, "tell me just *once* that I'm not taking this from you."

My fists tremble against the silk. I cannot let go. Your body grows cool and still in a way that has nothing to do with release. This time when you pull away, jeans around your knees, you peer out the dirty window and not at me. Now your voice is finally like I've always wanted it to be, just like the others: low and dangerous, threatening nothing I give a shit about losing. I can't even make out what you say, and I don't care.

I tug hard and the tie comes loose, silk disappearing between us as I drag you back down, back into me. I buck my hips to meet your thrusts, but my mouth is on yours, my arms around your neck. There is no struggle now except the struggle to bring you deeper. There should be words, wild promises and saying sorry, but I am coming before I even know it, your hand tight around me and a splash against your belly. At the feel of it, your sob echoes in the rented room, even louder than my own. It is not a sound of grief.

Eventually my fingers, still trailing silk, thread through your hair. I fight against using the scarf to wipe my eyes and snatch my cigs from the battered nightstand instead. Old habits die hard.

You press a kiss into my throat. "Thank you."

I swallow again, nodding. I can speak now, but there is no need.

You have already understood everything.

THE TAKING OF BRIAN KROWELL

Shane Allison

N ow or never. Do or damn die. I had fifteen minutes and counting before Brian's shift was up. I searched for a rock or a fake plant, a place I figured he would stash a key. I thought of the welcome mat, but would it be somewhere that obvious? Lifted it. There it was. He always was a presumptuous fuck. I couldn't believe he was still living in this dump, an apartment complex subject to flooding, gangs, hookers, and crackhead hustlers. He treated me to Hamburger Helper and old episodes of *Sex and the City* back when we were on speaking terms. I took the key and pressed it into the keyhole, walked in with my gym bag of goodies. His pad smelled lived in, faintly of hoagie sandwiches. The place was a wreck. How could he find anything in that mess? The guy works forty-hour weeks and he's still Dumpster-diving for hand-me-downs, salvaging sofas from other people's trash.

Time to put my plan into action. One wrong move and I was fucked. I made my way to Brian's bedroom, which was a war zone of dirty clothes. I sifted through his closet, piles of dirty unmentionables. Looked at my watch to check the time: 2:00 A.M on the dot. Not long now. I fished a nasty pair of underwear from the laundry basket—planned to use it to gag his sweet mouth. Brought the duct tape I borrowed from the toolbox on Daddy's truck. The stuff can take off a layer of skin if you're not careful. Scarred for life. I took my place inside the closet and waited for him. I was ready. This shit was going to be good. He was not going to be like the others. I had something special planned for his ass.

Within minutes I heard the screaming of hinges. I cracked the closet to watch. Brian threw his bag on the couch, flicked on the TV, the light in the kitchen. He talked to himself. He looked tired, but I didn't give a shit. Dick-tease didn't deserve my sympathy. Not after the way he reached in and fingered my heart. He made his way to the bedroom, sipping grape soda, kicking out of his shoes. I steadied myself, ready with a hanky laced with chloroform. I watched Brian undress, fingers making their way down a ladder of buttons on an ugly shirt till he was half-naked and bare-chested, showing stretch marks across love handles. He sat on the edge of the unmade bed to peel khakis off one ashy leg, then the other. White briefs hugged his ass. Beautifully. Cotton stretched across dark chocolate cheeks. My dick stiffened in my jeans. My palms were mitts of perspiration. My gums were salty and itchy with anticipation. My heart was a racehorse, sweat dripped from the pits inside my Polo pullover. He walked naked to the bathroom, flicked on the light, stood at the toilet. A tongue of piss rained. He flushed. I imagined tweaking his nipples, smearing my face across his big belly. His soft dick was peanut size. He pulled a pair of boxers from an open drawer.

Now. With his back turned, I lunged forward, out of the

closet, and pressed the chloroformed cloth hard over his face. He struggled, clawed at my arms and hands. His chewed nails couldn't break my skin. The drug knocked him out like a prize-fighter walloped by a haymaker. He was a fat, heavy, naked slab in my arms. I dragged him to the bed, tossed him on the tousseld sheets that smelled of ass and sweat. I rolled tongues of duct tape over his mouth, careful not to cover his eyes or nose with the heavy-duty adhesive. Then I used it to bind his wrists and ankles. He wasn't going anyplace. I locked the front door and closed the venetians. I killed the living room and kitchen lights. I was 'bout out of breath, my glasses were smudged. I made my way back to his naked brawn, stared at him. At Brian.

I recalled the day we met: two lowly English majors, enrolled in a playwriting class. He was different from the gold-chained, obsessed brothas I was used to seeing, the boys who bullied me in high school, called me a sissy in woodshop and a faggot in consumer math. Brian was nerdy, spoke like a white boy. He was pleasantly plump in all the right places. Thighs, gut, and a firm bubble-butt I wanted to sink my dick in. I always picked him to be in my plays and he went along. Until the roles turned gay, that is, when he declined. He didn't want the class to think he was a homo. So stupid. It was only a play. I had to scramble fast. A cute punk boy named Sam, a Korn fan with a piercing through his bottom lip, took Brian's place. We passed the class with just Cs, 'cause our instructor said none of our work was worthy.

I thought about Brian every day. Hardly made it through the semester. If he were gay, we'd have made the perfect couple. I channeled my love and lust for him into balled-up Kleenex and the creases of gay porno mags, composed erotic poems in tattered notebooks about sucking his dick, fucking his ass. When I thought to share a few verses with him, it broke my heart when he declared he didn't want to talk to me anymore, didn't want to hang out over cans of cherry soda and the good episodes of *Sex and the City*. I burned my journals with their covers of scarlet glitter hearts and swore there would be no more poems written about him. But the damage was done. I tried to call, only to be sent to the phantom zone of his voice mail. But I had to have him.

I gave him a swift whack across the ass. Dirty pup. It was the type of thing I liked using my hands for. It was time to take it out on his flesh, do with him whatever I wanted. I massaged his hips, kneaded brown-skinned fat. He was coming to. I reached for the chloroform, decided against it. He struggled to pull his wrists free from the tape.

"Be still," I told him, "or you're going to pull the skin." He whimpered, panted, soiled the tape across his mouth with snot and tears. His cries were useless. My dick was hard. I rubbed it through stretched denim. I didn't want him to see my face, so I ripped off a piece of the bedspread and blindfolded him. I mounted him and whispered, "Shhh, stop all this mess now. It'll be over soon." I applied more tape to his mouth, wrists, and ankles. Then I lifted myself off him, went into the bathroom. The lights were bright, burning my eyes. I searched the medicine cabinet for something to rub on my dick, to slather up his asshole. Just rubbing alcohol and citrus-flavored cough medicine. Next I checked the kitchen, searched the cabinets; there were all the usual condiments, mustard, herbs, spices. In the fridge: relish, chocolate syrup, grape jelly, fat-free salad dressing. I've used it all 'cept jelly. I grabbed the jar, returned to Brian's bedroom, set it on the bedside table, unscrewed the lid. I pulled my jeans down around my ankles, my underwear stained with shit streaks was pulled tight across my legs. The stench of crotch musk permeated the room. I left on my shirt. The leather ring around my balls kept my stuff erect. I dipped three fingers into the jar of artificially flavored jelly, slathered it between Brian's half-moons. He winced at my cold touch. With the tape double-layered, his screams were muffled.

"Hush now," I whispered. He had himself to blame.

Gobs of jelly dripped onto the floor, dark purple clumps. The sweet smell mixed with the pubic stink of Brian's ass and crotch. I scooped more jelly and applied it to my dick. Stuff was cold as shit. I slipped a finger into Brian's ass. He bucked. The jelly matted my pubic hair, pinches of pain as I stroked my hard-on.

Brian's body was tense with fear, and shivering with...excitement? I pulled my shirt over my head, took hold of his shoulder with one hand, aimed my dick at his hole with the other, and slid it in easily, thanks to the grape jelly oozing from his hole, and fucked him, my muscles aching from tension and desire. I reached under him for his dick. It was harder than mine. I'd take pleasure later, blowing it. His ass was a dream. My dream. At last. I wasn't worried about what I was doing. Raped men never tell. And I knew how to find him. I felt myself close to coming. Usually it takes me time to pop, but taking Brian for the first time, his bound body mine, was beyond exciting. I pulled out slowly, held my dick above his ass, shot thick streams of white fire across the dark skin of his back. I plunged a single finger in again, brought it to my lips, sucked shit and jelly from the digit. But I wasn't done with him. I wanted to know what a nerdy boy's dick tasted like. I checked the security of my flower-printed blindfold. It was holding. I rolled him over, his back stained with my spunk.

Brian's dick, circumcised, no longer the size of a peanut, curved slightly as it jutted toward the ceiling fan above us, where I could see blades caked with dust. A dew of sweat soaked his face, throat, torso. I reached into the jelly jar again. Two fingers full. I dabbed it onto his cockhead, ran my fingertips along his hot shaft. The roof of my mouth was dry. I tickled his cockhead with my tongue. So sweet. I sucked him clean, twisted his nipples. His dick tensed in my mouth, beyond my tenacious lips, cum surging through his black body, willing or not. Now I played with his balls, with his jelly-matted ball sac hair, then back to his nipples, harder, and his dick jerked, spasmed, and I gorged on his semen, swallowing.

I left him stained with his cum, my cum, my spit, his jelly. Done. His never was my now.

AND SERPENT BECAME ROD

Shanna Germain

I hadn't gotten it up in six weeks. Out in the jungle, it seemed at least I wasn't the only one; everything there struggled to rise, to defy the odds, defy the warm wet air. Everything struggled to come upright, to stay the course of forward motion. Or of any motion at all. Even me, putting one foot in front of the other, watching for the leaf-cutter ants beneath my feet, trying to discover the fuzzy-backed sloths in their hidden tree-spots.

Ahead of me, Jesus's voice floated down, pressing with its heavy rolled Rs and its constantly changing landscapes of lilts and valleys. He kept forgetting to hold the branches after his passing, and they whipped my face and shoulders with their sweating leaves, but I barely noticed. Volcanic ash layered itself on the skin between my boots and my shorts, burying the hairs on my legs.

I worked out at the gym back home every day, but that had not prepared me for this climb. I wanted to whine like a little kid, "Are we there yet?" But I had paid for this privilege, this hope, so I kept my lips closed against the smack of the branches and kept climbing, taking some sort of pleasure in watching the long muscles in Jesus's calves, the way his ass moved beneath his khaki shorts. It didn't stir anything in my cock or in my head. But I was hoping that would change soon.

I'd heard about this trek online. Like so many other things that passed along through the intangible Web, it didn't seem real. Not possible. But if it was...how could I resist? I'd done everything else. I had enough money to buy my way into the most exclusive clubs, to hire the best tops. I had a roomful of equipment. Men who would gladly give up their evenings to bind me in whatever way I asked of them. And yet. And yet, my orgasms had started to feel like they weren't part of me anymore, something that happened in a faraway town that you might read about in the morning. Then, this. A cock that no longer worked.

My doctor gave me the "You're almost forty years old. This is to be expected" line and slipped me a prescription for something that would increase the blood flow to my cock. But I knew that wasn't the problem. It was something bigger, something deadening that had happened, so much that I could barely feel.

I wanted to come back with my erection restored. But I was hoping for much more than that.

If I made it up the damn volcano, that was. Jesus moved more like animal than man through the trees and up the steep slope. My legs were turning to river water. My mouth to desert. The "cool-dry" fabric that I'd spent too much money on was plastered to my chest and back with sweat. Every break in the canopy meant some breeze, but also more sun.

A slithering movement below my feet made me start. My heart, already working too hard, cranked up the speed until it felt like one singular beat in my chest. I uttered a short, high-pitched squeak. Even as the sound left my mouth, I realized the movement was a small green snake, no bigger around than my pinky. It swept its way across the trail until it reached the underbrush, plants with leaves the same color as its skin.

Jesus was watching me. "Is it true you are afraid of a snake?"

"No," I said, too quickly. Jesus didn't move his eyes away. Those brown eyes, so dark they were almost black, with long lashes that curled up like dark smoke. I wished he would lay me down in the middle of this jungle, force me to lick the sweat from his neck, the small of his back, that perfect space behind his balls. Such a soft boy's face in a man's body. I'd learned not to judge; some of the best tops I'd seen were small, nearly dainty in their bearing. And then there was me: power businessman, six foot plus, wanting nothing more than to be the perfect sub.

"I'm not afraid of snakes," I said. "It just...I wasn't expecting it."

Jesus kept watching me. "You do know where you're going, yes?"

I nodded until he seemed satisfied. He turned and I followed him up the trail in silence.

At the next clearing, Jesus stopped in front of me so quickly I nearly ran him over. "Here," he said. "We are here."

He pointed. A small building on the side of the mountain—volcano, really. It was a shack. Worse. Not much larger than an outhouse, less structurally sound.

"There?" My hope evaporated in the heat. I'd expected rural, rustic. I had been warned, but really.

Jesus looked at me the way he'd done on the trail, and I had that urge again. I wondered what his mouth would taste like.

"There," he said. "Good luck." He turned back toward the trail.

"You're leaving me here?"

"He works alone," Jesus said. He didn't look back.

"How will I get home?" The trail had seemed clear enough to follow up, but I suspected that it wouldn't be as easy to find on the way down.

"I will come at dawn," he said. "If you are here, I will lead you back."

"Dawn? If?"

He had already gone, stepping into the mouth of the dark woods that swallowed him up.

I waited, thinking the man might come out of his hut, that I might not have to go in. But no one appeared. Sunlight moved closer, flicked the corners of my shoulders with its long yellow tongue. Insects so small I wasn't sure I could see them flitted and buzzed near my eyes.

I walked to the shaded side of the hut, knocked on the door.

"Come." The accent wasn't Spanish. Something European, maybe? I couldn't be sure.

I pushed the door open. Candlelight flickered in every corner. The room was larger than I expected. And then I realized, no, it was the mirrors. Everywhere. Making a million candles, a million rooms. And between them all, tucked into doors and windows and walls, sat baskets and cages. The faint rustling inside each combined together, amplified like the candles. The sound sent a small shiver up my spine.

In the center, on a small chair, sat the man I'd come to see. A white man, which surprised me, I don't know why. His shaved head was bent, looking at something in his lap, and he wore a robe of brown cloth. Even sitting, he was a long man, with long bones and long muscles.

"You're Nagari?" The surprise showed in my voice even though I hadn't meant it to.

The man nodded without looking up. "I am."

I stood there, uncertain. The room smelled of skin and sweat and animal. Not unpleasant, but earthy. Primal.

I reached into my shorts pocket for my wallet, but he waved a hand. "This is not about money," he said.

I let the wallet fall back into my pocket, but didn't close the flap. When was anything not about money?

The silence between us was filled with the flare of candles, the slow rustle of things moving in the dark. "I'm ready to start," I said.

Finally, he looked up. Even in the candlelight, his eyes flickered green. He was younger than I'd thought, too. No spiritual guru here, I realized. Probably just a man they hired for suckers like me. How many men bore the name of Nagari and sat in this hut, I wondered? How many American dollars passed hands in this small, dark space?

"No," he said. "You are not ready until I say you are ready." His gaze turned back to his hands as though I wasn't there, as though I'd never been there at all.

A feeling flickered in the space below my belly. At first, I clocked it as anger. How fucking dare he? Didn't he realize—

And even as I started to rant, I realized that the small sideways movement was desire. Hope. I couldn't remember the last time a top wasn't the least bit afraid of me, a binding that hadn't been loosened by my standing, a blow that hadn't been softened by what money could buy.

My cock didn't respond, but my heart did. *Thunk-thunk.* I waited, standing, my skin raining salt and water in the silent heat of hut and candles. My calves, already tight from the climb, began to ache and pull.

It was a snake that he was looking at, I realized, twining between his hands, his wrists. Black as a night without the city, without stars or moon. It coiled slowly, without sound, and he watched it. Grass growing. Molasses pouring. That was how slow.

I became impatient. I urged the snake forward, onward. My eyes adjusting to the semidark, I noticed things I hadn't before: the small black scales with their perfect shine, the length of the man's fingers, the stillness with which he sat. I slid into a state of watching, nothing beyond the movement of the snake, one scale forward, a centimeter and inch. Time was marked only by a knuckle covered, and finally, a second one.

So intent was I, I barely realized that he, too, was moving. Standing, snake still wrapped around one arm. For all the length of his bones, he was only as tall as me, but with power and deliberation in his movement. The robe slipped from his shoulders as he came forward, sliding down to puddle at his feet. His body, so pale, was covered with dark tattoos: snakes and scales and words that I couldn't read. The live snake around his wrist, another around his ankle. His cock, the long slim length of it, uncoiled from its nest.

I bowed my head before him.

"Undress," he said.

I did so, slipping off my clothes without looking up. It felt good to be free of them, to stand on the dirt floor of the hut in my bare feet and feel the cool of the earth through my soles. Still, I was ashamed of my own cock, the soft-shelled egg of it, a fragile broken thing.

I kept my head bowed, my eyes on the dark floor beneath my feet. Nagari came close enough that I could smell him, that primal earth, that dark animal power. He took my wrist with the snake hand, held me there. I felt the first touch of the dark scales. The cool roughness of the body made my skin flinch and twitch like an animal's.

I started to pull back—instinct—something deeper than I understood. At the movement the snake raised its head, sudden and strong, sent its black tongue into the air. Lulled and seduced by its slow crawl, I hadn't expected it could move so fast.

"They are skittish," he said. "Easily agitated. Prone to bite, not flight. No poison, but teeth all the same."

The snake opened its mouth. I couldn't see teeth, but I believed they were there. I knew that I was shivering, couldn't seem to control the way my body trembled.

"Be still," he said. I'd heard so many ways to say that; so many commands to stop moving, to bow, and yet not one had the power of his simple words.

I tried to obey. I stilled my body so all I could feel was the thump of my pulse in my wrists and neck and thighs. After a minute, he let the snake slide entirely from his wrist, wrap itself around mine. The snake settled in, tightened against the warm pulse of my blood. Its small tail slipped between my fingers, wagged like a cat's against my skin. I tasted fear or desire in the roof of my mouth. I couldn't tell the difference.

Nagari let go of my arm and moved away, among the cages and baskets. He came back with a second snake, larger than the first. It wound its way across my other arm, not content to stay at my wrist, instead sliding to my elbow, coiling in the crook. They weren't heavy, but I felt the weight of their power and speed and the weight of Nagari's green-gold eyes in the candlelight.

He moved around me, silent as the snakes themselves, taking them from their cages and unleashing them at ankle and knee. They honed in to my pulse points like dogs to the kill. Whether it was the warmth or the movement they were seeking, I didn't know. I only knew to stand still, to give myself over to the cool weight of them.

One found its home along the crook of my shoulders, at the base of my neck. It didn't constrict, although I feared it would, just wound itself around, tight and black as a leather collar. I had to raise my head from bowing to breathe. With every exhalation, I felt the pulse of my fear, my desire, beat its way out.

Nagari stood before me, holding a small black snake by the tail. Smaller than that one I'd seen on the trail earlier, it writhed and swarmed. I was afraid of its tiny black tongue, the way its head moved back and forth, the blind seeking. He held out his other hand, a pinkie, and the snake slithered up and wrapped itself around. A ring of ebony and tongue.

Nagari knelt before me without giving the impression that he was kneeling. He did it by keeping his eyes locked to me, by keeping his power over me.

"And here," he said.

Surprised, I let go of his stare to look down, at my cock uncoiling from its sheath, lifting its head to meet his hand.

My hands at my sides, wrapped in slow-writhing black, bound by ankle and knee and neck, I watched my cock crawl from its small basket and come to life. I had forgotten what it looked like, rosy-pink head ready to strike, the body shifting, lengthening forward into the air.

"Now," he said. "You are ready."

He unlooped the black ring from his finger like removing a curl, and rewrapped it at the base of my cock. A small, soft tightening like a rope pulled closed, and my cock jerked twice, rose higher toward my belly.

"Oh," I said, and the snake at my neck shifted its head behind my ear.

Each time the snake around my cock settled, I hardened, and the snake settled again.

Nagari rose. He, too, was harder than when I'd come in.

Devoid of any snakes other than his tattoos, he looked meaner and stronger. He leaned forward without touching me and licked the edges of my lips. I exhaled my pulse again, and he probed into that new space. What he tasted of, I couldn't say. Nothing I knew to put a name to. Exotic fruits or insects plucked from trees, the dirt and candlewick of the air, the salt and sweet of his tongue. He sucked my tongue into his mouth, eating my voice.

When he stepped back, I tried to follow. The snakes held me there with a raised head, the slip of a tail along the curve of my balls. Everything drew up tight. Still. I bowed my head as much as I could without losing my breath. I waited for the man that I knew would save me.

Finally, he touched me, my shoulder, my hip, the dark curls below my belly, his body slipped and rolled. Undulation. The snakes seemed to follow his motion, to move without moving. If I so much as leaned forward, the black body rings I wore tightened, loosened, scale-slipped along to a new place.

When he put the wet tips of his fingers to my cock, my eyes unfocused in the half-life, spelled shapes and shadows into things that weren't there. I rose for him. I let him trail around me, loop me with his fingers, sidewind his way up and down me until I worried that my knees would buckle, that I would fall into the dirt, snake-wrapped and writhing. His hand tightened, the snake at the base did the same, until I was surrounded by white and dark skins. Until I couldn't see anything except the rosy head of my cock, slick and shining in the candlelight.

He let me go, let my cock bob up to my belly in its wanting. From behind me, he put his lips to my ear. I could hear his breath, and the glide of the snake's head through my hair.

Something flickered at the crack of my ass. Snake tongue? Man tongue? I moaned, low in my throat.

"Still now," he said.

He bent me slow, from the waist, one vertebra at a time. The snakes stayed coiled, silent. His fingers spread my asscheeks, searching for entry to that hot, wet place inside me. I could only think of snakes entering burrows, even as he slid his finger all the way in and wiggled it inside me. Everything outside stopped as he began to work me with his fingers. The snakes slept against my skin, the candle flames sat straight and tall. Only my pulses moved, quick as mice, scampering their way to neck and wrist and cock.

He fingers left me and I knew what was coming. I wanted it, but I wasn't ready. I didn't think I was ready, so focused on cock and snakes and his lips against my ear.

"Wait," I said.

He didn't.

The first push and I hissed, leaned my tongue out and tasted my own lips.

The second push, I opened for him as though he'd unhinged me.

The third push, I sucked him in whole.

He put his hand on my cock and a long strip of pleasure started in my back and brain, worked its way down and up and sideways. He fucked me without moving me, without letting me move. Only my cock jumped inside his fist, precum shining on its dark head. What it felt like, I couldn't say, something I hadn't felt in too long. Letting go and holding on and intoxicated blood beating hard, flooding my body.

My fists clenched and the snakes at my wrists shimmied awake, raised their heads. My cock twitched, and Nagari's hand and snake constricted, milking the venom from me, sending the hot white spray into the dirt. As I came, my voice entered the room and the snake at my neck sank his teeth into the flesh of my ear.

Nagari pulled out of me and came seconds later, spraying the back of my heels. The snakes there twitched and pulled.

He unwrapped each snake as carefully as he'd bound me with them, slid each one back into its basket or cage. My ear and ass throbbed. My cock was still spitting out off-white droplets into the dirt. The smell came to me again, earthy and primal, but stronger now, muskier, and I recognized it for the sex-scent that it was.

When I was naked of the snakes, and Nagari wore his again, he handed me the pile of clothes I'd shed earlier. I took them, but they didn't feel like they belonged to me anymore. If I unfolded them, I knew I'd find a layer of my own skin there as well, opaque and empty of life.

Nagari pulled his robe on and sat back in his chair, his eyes once again on the snake at his wrist. I took my wallet from the pocket and put all the cash I had on top of one of the snake baskets. He didn't look up.

I stepped out of the shack and was surprised to find it was still daylight. My eyes watered against the bright of the sun. I put one hand over my eyes and laid my clothes next to the path. Then I moved forward in my new skin.

A GIFT TO THE RISING DOG STAR

David Holly

Day 57

Fifty-six nights had passed since my captors carried me to the house of Millo. His dwelling was a reddish edifice of two stories with walls of sun-baked mud, an emblem of its owner's accomplishment in trade. Consigned to the slaves' quarters, I wore a simple tunic and ate the coarse food. Only the slave Athaliah would talk to me. During the afternoon of my fifty-seventh day, she found me where I squatted against a smooth wall that was still cool in spite of the growing heat.

"Kareah," she said slyly, her derisive scorn ever present. "Your fate has been decided. Millo has consulted Ephraim, Sorcerer of the Chaldeans, who advised giving you to the Enaeriae."

"What are the Enaeriae?" I asked. I was not of this place, for Millo's marauders had stolen me from my home in a land far to the west. Thus far, my bondage had not been onerous, nor had any demands been made of me. Still, I was the proverbial stranger in a strange land and not master of my own soul.

Athaliah snickered at my ignorance. "The Enaeriae are the dog worshippers of the Owl Goddess Lilith, the Great Whore of the Hebrews. In their rituals, the Enaeriae priests take the place of the goddess when they assume the position of the ass or the dog."

"Those are all animals," I muttered, not comprehending.

Athaliah mocked me again. "You will soon appreciate my meaning, Kareah. I trust that the priestly ritual will gratify you—though neither our master nor the Enaeriae will trouble about your pleasures—or your pains."

Day 73

Nothing happened for many days after Athaliah told me that Millo had offered me to the priests, and I began to suppose that she had been false or misguided. However, on the seventy-third day of my captivity, two strangers arrived at the gate. Soon Athaliah summoned me to the courtyard. My master Millo was bowing obsequiously to two men seated beneath the frond shelter. Arrayed in many-colored raiment fringed with bells, their faces painted like owls, the men were swilling Millo's luxurious yellow wine and picking at bowls of dates, nuts, and honey cakes.

"Here is Kareah," Millo said. "Is this merchandise not as well-rounded as I promised?"

The two strangers were examining me as though I were the scape-ram selected for sacrifice to Azazel. "Let him be stripped of his tunic," one of the strange men spoke.

Millo directed two slaves to undress me. As I stood bare beneath the burning sun, I saw my only garment carried into the house, doubtless to cover the nakedness of Millo's next captive.

"Turn him," the second stranger demanded, and the slaves slowly revolved me for the men's inspection. After I had been turned twice, the strangers demanded, "Bend him." The slaves bent me, quite low, with my rear toward the strangers, and held me long in that humiliating pose. At last, the strangers acknowledged that the temple would be pleased to accept Millo's gift.

"Let the bequest be bound," the strangers decreed, and several slaves brought forth long hide strips that had been soaking in water for a week.

"No," I gasped, for I knew how the leather would bite as it dried and tightened.

The slaves laughed at my protests as they drew my arms behind me and fixed my wrists. Other thongs were tied around my chest, strung down to my crotch so they pulled my rod and stones close, and threaded between my buttocks. This latter binding gave me pain, and I complained bitterly, but the slaves only chortled as they bound my legs. Athaliah was one of those, and she whispered as she tied me. "Your manhood will no longer be of use to you, Kareah. Lilith will use you—in the guise of her priesthood—in the manner she sees fit." Athaliah winked as she added, "Your orifices shall substitute for the Great Whore's slit."

With that perplexing prediction reverberating through my thoughts, Athaliah slipped a sack over my head so that I could not see, nor even scarcely breathe, and the slaves tossed me helpless into the strangers' cart.

Day 91

As I squatted in pitch-black confinement, miserable with dread and despair, Azgad came for the final time and assured me that the night of my resurrection had arrived. I had been nine days like unto one dead, and having died to the world I knew, I could be reborn as Lilith's surrogate.

For two days after being carried from the house of Millo, I

rode in the back of a cart, bound and naked, hungering, burned by the sun, half-suffocated, afraid the ever-tightening bonds would stop my breath or blood. I heard the drivers talking about the Great Ziggurat that rose to Uranus and descended into Tartarus, though I could not then see the temple.

Unable to walk after my ordeal, I was carried behind walls of cyclopean stones. There, under the watchful eye of the acolyte whom I came to know as Azgad, young men washed me of my filth and gave me small bites of food. When I had eaten, they locked a leather collar around my neck, not so tight to strangle but not so loose to slip off. A leash fastened to the collar, so the young men could lead me like an ass or a dog. These young men concealed their genitals with leather breechcloths that threaded between their clefts and tied around their waists, but they kept me bare as the day I was born. Still, they calmed me, cleaned me, fed me, massaged me, and exercised me. Before many days passed, I regained the use of my muscles, and indeed, developed new ones where no bulge had existed earlier.

One day after an intense session of lifts designed to swell my buttocks, Azgad told me that my new birth would occur in nine nights. Until that time, I must reside in the house of Cerberus. Azgad hauled me, still unclothed, down a curving stair into the bowels of Tartarus. Deep down, we reached a cell, about six cubits around and four cubits high. A round hole in the floor gave to a foul cesspit. After Azgad had secured the end of my lead to a bronze hook sunk into the stone, he abandoned me to the terrifying darkness.

Lacking fire or knife, I lay curled in the unfeeling dark. Twice a day Azgad came, and I welcomed his arrival no matter what delights or horrors he brought. With a bladder attached to a hose, he flooded my bowels with scented oils and bid me release into the cesshole. Twice a day, I received three bags full of the warm olive oil. Then cleaned inside, I lay while Azgad washed me from head to toe. At the last, he fed me and gave me sweet water to drink. Once his tasks were completed, he abandoned me to the demon-haunted darkness until his next visit.

On his eighteenth visit, Azgad performed his customary ritual. However, after I had emptied my bowels and refreshed myself with food, he took a knife of bronze and sliced the lead at the iron ring. "Come, Kareah. Be born into the life of the Enaeriae," said he, and he hauled me up the steep curving stairs.

After my close confinement, the hall into which Azgad brought me was impossibly large. Crouched in shadow stood four altars, facing the directions of the wind, the mountains, the sea, and the fires. Torches and incense burned on the altars, and behind them stood four man-sized statues. One statue was ass headed, one dog headed, one owl headed, and the fourth was like unto no creature I knew. However, most remarkable about the statues were their immense jutting members, swollen for penetration into some orifice.

A fifth altar stood in the center of the hall, and to this Azgad led me and secured my lead. His tasks complete, Azgad slipped into the lowering shadows from whence came the sibilance of breath. A form then approached me. He bore the body of a man, virile, erect, and naked save for a harness of leather, but he had the head of an owl. I struggled to unfasten the lead, but hope of escape was futile. My heart raced until I comprehended that he was only a man wearing a mask. He wordlessly displayed a second mask designed to fit over a man's head. When he set the mask he was carrying upon the altar, I saw that it was the visage of a dog. The mask did not have holes for eyes, rendering its wearer blind, but it did have a round hole at the mouth. The significance of that opening did not occur to me then.

The priest then held a tall clay vessel filled with dark wine to my lips. Some grain was mixed into the wine, which thickened the drink, and it had a musky odor, but I drank it down. My mother had stirred poppy juice into wine to help me sleep, but the priest's wine tasted quite different from my mother's mixture.

When I had drunk fully, the priest took the dog mask and slipped it over my head. The mask felt very strange, and vibrant colors swirled before my eyes. I tried to lift the mask, which was making my skin crawl, but huge hands seized my shoulders and pulled me forward until I was sprawled across the altar. My wrists were quickly secured to two iron posts affixed for that purpose. Beyond all reasoning, I felt my rod hardening, and I was sorry that my hands were tied. I would surely have reached for it, rubbed it, fondled it, and pounded it until I spilled my seed—no matter how many priests might be watching. I felt a sexual heat coursing through my entire form, and thoughts such as I had never entertained before beat upon my mind.

"The first phase of your new birth begins," intoned a voice. "It is written that you, Kareah, shall serve the lusts of men in the stead of the Goddess. You will now taste the seed of the acolyte."

I had the sense of a man approaching me, standing near to my masked head. I could feel the heat of his loins. Then something large and smooth pushed through the mouth hole of my mask and brushed my lips. All unbidden, I opened my mouth to taste it, and it pushed in, gliding along my tongue until it reached the back of my throat. Perhaps the drink had stolen my reflex to gag, for the object seemed quite natural there, though naught else felt ordinary in my body or in my mind. My flesh was aflame with dry lust, and my mind was whirling with spiraling owls and running dogs and braying asses.

The object in my mouth pulled back to my lips, though I lapped it with my tongue on its way. When I caressed it with my lips, it slid forward again. A thin fluid was leaking from it, a tart but pleasant taste. I sucked harder, trying to extract more tasty fluid.

As I sucked on the treat, strong hands stroked my buttocks. The ghost of my father booming condemnation, I tried to hunch forward, but my straps held. The hands did not leave my buttocks, but caressed them more earnestly. Strangely, these caresses aroused me in a new and exciting way, and my father's ghost fled. My mind whirled with images of mating stags. I had once witnessed a male hart mount another male, penetrate his fellow anally, and hump him as he would a female. The male receiving the penetration did not resist—rather he behaved as if he enjoyed it.

As I sucked on the object sliding in and out of my mouth, I felt it stiffen and grow even harder. It throbbed atop my tongue; then it gave a sudden spasm and a copious amount of ambrosial nectar filled my mouth. Only after I had swallowed did the kaleidoscopically colored clouds swirling through my consciousness abruptly part so that I knew what I had done. I had sucked on the sexual rod of an acolyte, and I had drunk of his seed.

As the spent rod was drawn past my lips, the hands caressing my buttocks explored into my cleft. I wiggled my rump, deceiving myself that I was trying to escape violation, but down deep an inner voice hailed rapture. In my father's village, men were tossed over the precipice for such behavior. Still, I assured myself that I was blameless, being bound and masked, a captive, a stranger, a chattel to be bought, sold, and used by this or that will. Yet again the deep down inner voice spoke true—I was reveling in my ravishment, and the pagan mask, and the bonds, and the ritual narcotic I had so readily drunk were not responsible for the wanton lusts that rose from my own nature.

I wiggled my buttocks again in knowing invitation. "Take

me," I spoke aloud the words that filled my mind unbidden. Perhaps the priest was whispering them into my ear as I spoke, but I could not be certain. "Fill me. I offer my haunches to the Great Goddess Lilith. My rump shall henceforth be a fissure to satisfy the cravings of men to the glory of Lilith. My mouth shall henceforth be a hole to gratify the lusts of men to the bliss of Lilith. This I swear—forever."

"Receive the cleft stick." Hands parted my buttocks and I felt a small object inserted therein, a finger, perhaps, or some pleasure device. I opened easily for it, quite easily, for I heard snickers. I was too eager, and my zest amused the congregation.

"When I am high priest, I shall take men as they now do me," I muttered just before a second rod of flesh pushed into my mouth. Fighting my bonds, I feigned resistance, but even in feigning, I sucked. The bewitching cleft stick popped out of my hole, carving ripples of titillation through my whole being. Was it only the powerful drug producing my fascinating sensations, my disorder of senses, and my erotic hallucinations? Wild shifting colors swept across my masked eyes, and the masculine fluids I had consumed suffused the atmosphere with enticing scents and tastes. The mask rippled against my flesh so that my lips felt stung and swollen around the thick rod.

"Prepare, Kareah, you must submit to the priestly rod," a voice intoned.

Lilith must have smiled upon me; I could not speak above a moan of assent; else, I would have shouted, "Take me, bind me, lash me, use me as your dog."

The second rod exploded with seed in my mouth. Though I swallowed heartily, it withdrew and decorated my face within the dog mask. As the elixir of creation slid down my throat, a fresh insight made me shudder. The thoughts of the previous moment had not been my own; the drugged wine had caused my illusion of empowerment. The bonds holding me abruptly grew tighter, and my abject helplessness overwhelmed me. I was only a captive, a slave—my body was not my own—my private places were not my own. Any man could enter me or abuse me as he willed, and I was powerless.

A cry escaped me and I thrashed within my bonds. As I struggled, I felt a thick rod pushing against my anal cleft. "Kareah, your delivery has come, whore of Lilith," intoned the speaker. "Look now upon your brotherhood."

I moaned with yearning trepidation as the acolytes pulled the mask from my head, and I witnessed the congregation indulging in a frenzied orgy. The flames rising before the statues revealed men plugged into the crevices of other men, thrusting, grunting, howling praises to the painted image of Lilith upon the wall, and collapsing after blasting their seed into the bowels of their targets. The lurid walls threw up images of male submission to the power of the unimaginable invaders. I knew then that I would never rise to become one of those exalted beings who live to penetrate: I was ordained to be a mere acolyte, one of the penetrated, my flesh serving only to fulfill, to absorb, to provide a hole for the covetousness, privilege, frustration, and lunacy of men—for as long as I should live.

With that revelation reverberating wildly through my consciousness, I felt the rod of my duty pushing into my rear hole. I opened wider and wider, and as the thickness slid into me, a rapturous ecstasy followed. A deep, rich sensation rippled up my fissure as the rod of the priest drove deeper, those nectar-enhanced hallucinations of touch escalating my groaning pleasure.

As the priest's loins at last crushed my rounded buttocks, a deep series of thrills rippled through my crevice. Continuing beyond imagining, the ripples turned into dark waves of delight so that my own stiff, tormented member bucked against the stone altar, and I blasted my seed. Drugged and bound, I shook with wild spasms as my anal hole performed its duty. I wriggled upon the hard and thick member—obediently—submissively—like the seed-hole of the disturbing goddess I had just become.

Day 986

Straps of hide bound me, my forearms to my thighs, while the fastenings around my elbows tied me to the priest Melchizedek behind me. As an acolyte of the lesser orders of the Enaeriae, it was my function and obligation to skewer my fissure upon Melchizedek's masculine stiffness and to provide a holy receptacle for his mannish moisture. At the rising of the Dog Star, worshippers had assembled even from Zoar and from beyond the Slime-Pits in the Vale of Siddim to watch us present the ritual of the Owl-Goddess.

The torches were burning high, illuminating the lurid walls, which seemed to shift and writhe, a chimera associated with the sacred drink we consumed. The close, hot atmosphere was rich with the sacred smoke, scented and heady, and the drummers had been pounding their instruments for hours until the heartbeat of the congregation had become one with the frenzied pulses of we who must complete the divine orgy.

The coarse members of the four statues had been painted red, and dripped with suggestive white fluid. The illustrated walls told a tale of plunging priests taking squirming acolytes in the mouth or in the cleft, goat-shaped hairy dwarves rutting twisting initiates, and great owl demons thrusting into the willing and the unwilling alike. Finally, dominating the scene, head tossed back and lips curled in the throes of orgasmic rapture, lolled the Great Whore of the Cosmos, taking pleasure from the sexually frenzied thrusting of priests and the bound wriggling of acolytes. Thus tied in front of my priest, bent, hunched, impaled upon his rod, my thoughts rampant with hallucinations of sight, sound, taste, touch, and scent, I, Kareah, writhed upon the priestly flesh that drove my own hard rod into sexual transport and reveled as I received the seed of Melchizedek in homage to the Eternal Mysteries.

BOUND
BY LOVE

William Holden

I awoke with a start. Jake was sitting on the edge of my bed, once again watching me. His eyes never left mine. He wore a pair of latex shorts and nothing else. His stomach and chest were covered in a thick blanket of dark curly hair. A tiny dumbbell pierced his left nipple. My cock responded with a twitch. His dark, green eyes glowed in the dimly lit room. My visual tour of his body stopped at the sight of a most incredible bulge building in his crotch, straining against the tight latex. He rubbed my left leg. His touch excited me as nothing had in a very long time.

Without so much as a word, he brought my left foot from underneath the covers. First he massaged it. Then he raised my foot to his face and sucked each toe, one at a time. His hand moved farther up my leg. My cock was swelling, wanting to be touched and caressed. I started to speak, but he quickly moved his hand to my mouth to stop me.

"Don't say anything, not a word." He leaned forward and

buried his tongue deep in my mouth. I could taste my own skin on his tongue.

He pushed his body on top of mine. His hardness pressed deep into my groin. I wanted to touch his body, to explore mysteries I hadn't yet uncovered, but his hands held mine in place. He was heavy against me.

Cold metal snapped against one wrist, then the other. Blood rushed to my heart. Jake shifted his body down my legs. I kicked, but not enough for him to notice. He sat on my left leg and placed a leather restraint on my right ankle, then reversed his position. I was helpless. My cock throbbed. I was as sexually charged as I had ever been.

"There, that's better. Don't you agree?" A curious smile crept across Jake's face. "I know this is what you've been wanting. I could see it in your eyes the last few times we had sex." He traced the edge of my cock with his finger, sending shocks of electricity through my body. "Why didn't you say anything? You know I'd do anything for you."

The drawer to the nightstand was half-open. He reached for a blindfold and a ball gag. He fit the gag on me quickly, expertly. My eyes pleaded with him to stop, then I could not see. I heard him leave.

Time crawled. Damp with my own sweat, the blindfold pressed into my eyes, blue and purple dots danced in my darkened vision. My cock was aching with sexual tension. I wanted desperately to touch it for release. But Jake knew, probably better then I did, what I really wanted. He was controlling my every move. The loss of any sense of time and space played games with my mind. I was sure he was standing next to me. Could I hear him breathe? I waited for his touch. I trembled with anticipation and fear—but no one was there. I wanted Jake more than ever. I needed desperately to be touched, anything but to be left alone.

I have no idea how long I *was* alone, maybe as little as thirty minutes, as long as several hours. Finally I heard footsteps, real ones. The bedroom door creaked opened. I heard noises so familiar…but in this situation, so foreign. Then, an odor, tantalizingly familiar. What was it? Sulfur. He was striking a match. Panic seized me. I pulled on the straps binding me to his bed.

The blindfold was pulled off. Jake stood next to me—naked, his stiff cock jutting from the dense patch of his black pubic hair. A thick layer of foreskin, already slick with his precum, covered the head of his cock. A candle flickered on the nightstand. Jake sat next to me.

"You know, I've never understood what you see in Gary. Don't get me wrong, I love my little brother. But, honestly, he's so severe in his belief that sex should be nothing but beautiful and gentle." He patted my cheek, lightly. "You and I both know how sex should be. That's why you started this affair with me, right?" He gazed at me, as if awaiting an answer, indifferent to the gag still firmly set in my mouth. "Well, not to worry. If I have to take a second seat to Gary, at least I can be seated there with you."

I watched as he moved over to the dresser and pulled out a pair of scissors. I was light-headed from fear, from the rush of blood through my body. He walked back to the bed. "Perhaps if Gary saw you differently, things might change for the two of you." Jake took the scissors and began to cut my shirt, starting from the bottom. My body trembled with each brush of the cold metal blades. He snipped slowly and carefully toward my neckline. With my chest partially exposed, he brought his face closer. He licked my nipples, starting with the left, first caressing and then biting it. He shifted to the right. I shivered as his teeth nipped my skin. The scissors began their assault on the sleeves. Before long my shirt lay in pieces on the floor.

Jake stretched out next to me, pressed his wet cock against my leg, and, slowly thrusting his hips, fucked my leg. His tongue washed my sweaty armpits. He moaned with pleasure. He stroked my naked torso with the cold scissors. Jake was lost in his own world. The edge of one of the blades grazed my right nipple. The pain was instant. The gag blunted my attempt to yell out his name. The scissors came to rest on the waistband of my briefs. I was mad with desire. I wanted him, but couldn't have him. He wasn't allowing me that privilege.

The blades started again, cutting into my briefs. They slowly moved down my crotch, cutting into the white cotton. My swollen balls contracted at their cold, steely touch. With my underwear gone, Jake tossed the scissors aside and made his way to my dick. His mouth was warm. His tongue fondled bulging veins. I moaned, thrusting my cock into his mouth, my orgasm building.

He pulled my dick from his mouth. I shivered in the cool air as his spit ran down the shaft. He lowered himself to my balls and chewed on the skin, almost as if it were gum. His large hands covered my ass, gripped buttcheeks, squeezed. His fingernails dug into my skin. He raised my body off the sheets, just enough to allow his tongue access to my tight, pink hole. I gripped the headboard, my muscles stretched to their limit, tensing even more as his tongue slipped into my ass, fucking me with its wet strength, deep inside of me, before withdrawing to move up my torso, licking precum that had oozed from my cock—where a hot load of cum was building—and the sweat from my body. He removed the gag and kissed me, giving back my fluids mingled with his own saliva. He sat on my chest, his enormous cock gripped in his hand. He rubbed his wet foreskin across my lips.

"Now it's time to get you ready." He lifted himself off and

left the room. I called for him. No reply. My arms ached as my muscles tightened even more from wrestling against the restraints that were stretching me. My hard cock lay motionless against my stomach, the veins a deep purple from their frustrated workout. My balls felt as if they were in a vise. When Jake reappeared, he held a leather pouch.

"Gary's told me how much he loves your hairy body." He laughed briefly. "You know, it's odd. For years Gary has talked to me about your sex life. How amazing it is and how much you both get into each other. I believed him, I had no reason not to, but I never saw you as the plain Jane of the bedroom. There was always a hidden passion in your eyes. I was right the entire time. You weren't sexually happy with my little brother. How could you be?"

It was true. Every word. And it took being bound to Jake's bed for me to realize it. I would always love Gary. Nothing would ever change that. But it was Jake that I desired sexually. They were complete opposites. Jake worked out and had the most amazing sculpted body. His black hair was shoulder length and dusted with gray. There was a masculine quality to him, that drove me crazy, a quality that Gary, the slim, hairless brother, would never possess.

As I lay there, comparing the two brothers, Jake unzipped the pouch. He brought out a small can of shaving cream, a smaller pair of scissors, and a straight razor. He laid them out on the bed methodically. He left the room once again, and returned with a small basin of water and a damp cloth. He wiped down my armpits and smeared them with a dab of shaving cream. I trembled as the straight razor made its way across each pit, clearing the thick hair. The exposed skin burned.

Once my armpits were hairless, Jake made his way to my chest. He washed every inch of my torso with the warm washcloth, and rubbed in the mint-scented shaving cream. I already missed my body hair; I had always enjoyed how Gary played with it, how it was soaked after sweaty sex. I was angry with Jake. I wanted to scream at him to stop. Except that my cock was responding with every stroke of the blade.

With my chest bared, he turned with the small scissors to my dark bush of pubic hair, trimming carefully and patiently. The look on his face was pure concentration and pleasure. The muscles around my ass contracted when his attention turned to my hairy crack. Before long my body was hairless, nothing left but skin reddened by the razor's edge.

Jake looked up at me, obviously pleased with his own work. "That's much better. Don't worry about the red spots. They'll disappear soon enough." His eyes were gleaming with lust. He sat for a few moments, running his eyes over my body, nodding in approval. Then he straddled me. The hair on his balls chafed my tender skin. His foreskin was wet with precum. He smiled as he reached behind him, found my cock and began to squeeze it. His grip became stronger, bringing tears to my eyes. My cock-head swelled. He rubbed the head of my cock over his hole. With one downward plunge, his tight, hairy ass swallowed my cock. He sat with a look of triumph on his face. He reached toward the nightstand and grabbed the candle. With the candle in one hand and his own cock in his other, he began to ride my shaft.

The feel of him was incredible. He tightened his ass muscles around my cock and pumped harder. My balls throbbed as he pounded my cock. But I kept my eyes on that candle. It began to tip. A drop of hot wax beaded up on the rim. Then the first drop hit my right nipple, a shock wave of pain and pleasure. As the wax hardened, my nipple pulled tight. The next drop splashed onto my left nipple. He rode me deeper. The third drop singed my stomach—and I lost my load inside him. He moaned with pleasure as wave after wave flooded his ass. Within seconds I felt the hot rush of his cum on my face. I licked what I could off my lips; the rest ran down my cheeks. A second round of his hot liquid covered my chest. He collapsed onto me, his weight forcing out what little breath I had left.

I was in the bathroom, surveying my hairless body. My cock lengthened as I thought of Jake and our morning together. Gary called to me from our bed. My stomach knotted as I thought about him lying there waiting for me. How was I going to explain this? I slipped on a T-shirt and a pair of sweatpants, my vain attempt at covering up. I took a deep breath to calm my nerves and stepped out of the bathroom.

Gary was in bed, the sheets pulled up to his hips. The edge of his pubic hair poked out from the material; his cock hidden just beneath was erect. I walked to my side of the bed and crawled in.

"Why are you wearing those clothes?" He scooted closer to me.

"I'm a little cold." I turned my head to kiss him good night and rolled over on my side. He moved his body next to mine. His cock pressed into the crack of my ass. He felt warm. His hand reached around my torso and pulled me closer. He kissed the back of my neck. I closed my eyes and thought of his brother. I prayed he wouldn't touch my hairless skin as his hand moved down my chest. His fingers played with the edge of my T-shirt. His hand moved under the material. He stopped, sat up in bed and looked at me. He grabbed my shirt and pulled it up. He was emotionless as he looked at my body.

Our eyes met. He saw me remembering Jake.

NUMBER TWENTY-FOUR

TruDeviant

I hurry into the men's room. It's huge, at least fifteen standard urinals in a row and a couple of stalls to the side. Guys are lined up in front of every one of them, six or seven deep. Most of them are wasted on Miller Lite. Some are beyond wasted: demolished.

Several of the most fucked-up ones have their dicks out already and are pissing on the litter-strewn concrete floor, while they holler and laugh and forget that they shouldn't look at each other's cocks for more a half second. The testosterone hanging between their legs is as thick as the sting of fresh hot beer piss in the air. It's a strange and welcome contrast to the odor of over-cooked hot dogs, which I just left outside the door.

I cut in front of a couple of these bawdy toilet dudes and let out my own powerful surge of pale liquid into the gaping porcelain mouth. Feels so good. There are at least a couple of those big paper cups full of cheap beer flowing out of me. I look down and see the lemony water splash back on my blue jeans when it hits the little drain holes I'm aiming for.

I can't help but think of you, continuing to add detail to the thoughts I was having about you minutes ago. Day after day, I've stared at those pictures of you on my computer monitor. I've changed the color of your uniform. I've taken away the shadows on your face. I've removed the other guy's hand as it covers part of your arm. I've made the grass a brighter green. I've blurred the faces of the fans. Only you are identifiable.

I've made you perfect.

I've retouched maybe a hundred electronic images of you over the last five years to make you look good on those trading cards. But I don't count them or the thousands of images of your teammates and opponents. I never get past your number, number twenty-four.

Who would've thought that I'd be here tonight with you? You're only a few hundred feet away from where I was just sitting in the crowd.

I won the last and biggest lottery at work. The one that all the jocks wanted to win: the World Series. The face value of both tickets together is three hundred dollars. I saw the faces of all those guys as I walked back to my desk with the tickets in my hand, all of those baseball fanatics who would pay twice that amount to go to this game. Most of them were fuming because I got them, a few scheming how to get their hands on them.

It's just not fair, is it? Just not fair that the faggot won them. The faggot who, after five years, still doesn't know which player's name goes with which face and which team everyone belongs on. The faggot you guys try either to avoid in the john at work by going into a stall to pee, or else go to great lengths to show him your dick. The dick you're just so sure that he wants to get down on his knees for and suck and suck and suck until all of those potential two-point-five children of yours go shooting down his throat.

It's even worse that the faggot is really going to the game and has no intention of asking any of you to go with him. Not that any one of you could really accept the invitation. Well, maybe you could make an ultraspecial exception just for this one thing. But since he's not going to offer, you can confidently say you'd never go with him to the game.

Now I'm back in my seat. It's the start of the eighth inning. You are running out on the field.

I'm glad I scalped the other ticket before I came into the stadium. I could've asked a friend, but I don't want to be distracted from you, to share you with anyone I know. In the middle of this rowdy crowd of strangers I can have you all to myself.

I bet I'm not the only one here among the fifty-six thousand fans in Yankee Stadium who is having at least some form of erotic fantasy about one of the players. Even now, you're bending over as you do every inning before the enemy comes up to the plate. You're stretching out the tendons and muscles in your legs. Your butt is pointed directly at me, just a hundred feet or so away. I know it's a fine butt, so firm under those uniform pants. You move it up and down for me as I watch. I wish you would turn your head around and see me looking at your ass.

This game is nearly won. Your opponents feel the voracious pressure of this coliseum crowd beating them down. Soon you will be with all your teammates near home plate. You will come all over yourselves with the fermented froth of champagne and touch each other in the only way men like you can touch each other intimately. Hands briefly on each other's asses. Wet, hard embraces broken by frenetic backslapping. A kind of laughter and yelling, strangely similar to the pixilated version of manly display I just witnessed in the toilet. A joyous, sensual, yet sexless Roman orgy.

I can see myself as one of the Braves, the quashed Atlantian

Indians, a couple of feathers on my head, looking through the bush at the white men, who are unaware that a straggler has escaped their guns and the diseases. Or maybe I'm a Southern-fried soldier stumbling onto the Yankee regiment that just defeated my Dixieland comrades in a downhill battle.

No! Tonight I am just myself, the atypical fan who appreciates you for reasons other than your contribution to the sweep of the century. I've been scrutinizing your image for five years, and you still remain the enemy.

Yes, we are enemies. I can never have you unless I force you, even in this fantasy.

So I sneak into your locker room. The others have conveniently gone ahead to an after-victory celebration. You've had a few swigs of that champagne before opening your locker. You sit on the narrow bench in front of it and kick off your sneakers. The scent merges with the already powerful stench of sweat around you. I move in behind you. You stand up and turn around to face me with questions in your eyes.

I gut punch you, a short hard jab that knocks all the air out of your lungs and, as you jerk toward me, your cap falls off your head. The short black hair is wet underneath. You rasp and fall forward into my arms. Mouth open. I see your pink tongue. I feel the coarseness of your polyester jersey on my bare hands as your full weight hits me and almost topples me.

I smell the champagne on you and mixed with your breath. I have an impulse to touch your lips. Their embossed edges hover so close to my lips, while your darkening eyes are wide with confusion. I let go of you and you slip slowly down to the cement floor. You are gasping for breath, like a barracuda that suddenly finds itself in the bottom of a boat.

I quickly yank out a coil of rope from my backpack, tie your wrists together, and toss the rest of the rope over the metal beam above your head. In a moment you are standing in front of me, just starting to really struggle. You're finally breathing in little gulps of air with less difficulty. I loop each ankle and tie the cord to the wooden feet that support the lockers on either side of you.

And there you are: spread-eagled and not much room for struggling in comfort, even if you could breathe normally. I waste no time. I move right up to you. Press against you, my beat-up leather jacket and faded jeans against your white pin-striped uniform. I lick your lips. You sputter and try to jerk around. My hands are on your ass, pulling you into me. You are trying to yell, to curse, but you can't even do that.

Again I lick your lips. You try to bite my tongue. The hate in your eyes is horrible, but somehow satisfying to me, your captor who has wanted you from so far away for so many years now.

I pull out a roll of PVC tape from my gym bag. I wind some around your head, cover those pretty lips, and put those dangerous teeth of yours away. You snort as you struggle to get air into your nose. Snot flies out onto my jacket. I slap your face, just hard enough to get your attention. You resume your struggling with more intensity. I stay close to you. I feel your hard body moving against mine.

I've felt a number of hard bodies over the years, but somehow that dirty wet uniform separates you from all the others now that I'm touching you in it. Without looking down I know how it fits every part of your body. I know where the cloth wrinkles, how it bunches up at your crotch and the crack of your ass, the bends in your arms and legs.

The hardness inside my briefs is unbearable, but I don't want to let go of you to free myself. I wonder if you could possibly be hard there beneath that jockstrap, which holds in all the spicy smell you've been collecting there during the game. But I know you aren't hard, yet.

Here we are, cocks pressed together, yours buried under all those layers of heavy, stinky cloth. Your uniform pants are stained with reddish dirt and green grass on the knees and a large smear of the same colors runs down the front of your jersey.

I grind into you. You grunt, nose still hissing air in and out. I smell your pits. They stink better than I imagined, though the polyester doesn't hold the stench like those old wool uniforms used to. I smelled the pits of a few of those uniforms in high school, pits discolored by the generous perspiration of young athletic competitors.

I feel your heart palpitating in your broad chest. I know you have a hairy chest. I've seen so many images of your furry arms. I keep rubbing the tense muscles of your shoulders through the thick material. Double knit polyester has this amazing feel when there is so much hard athlete standing in it, giving it its special shape.

When this fantasy first came to me, I made sure you were bound in a humiliating position. Much more embarrassing than your stance in the fantasy I hold of you now in my mind. The methodical jabbing rape of that hot ass: yeah, I played that one over so many times while jerking off in my bed.

Often there was some heavy ass whuppin' before and after those pants came down. Sometimes, other torments preceded and followed the taking of your ass. Sometimes, my silver knife, inlaid with onyx and turquoise, cut away your uniform and ended up with the blade resting on your Adam's apple.

But no, not now, not this time, at the moment of deepest fantasy—even as you stand there on the green in front of me— my revenge is sweeter than that. I will force you, but in a way that leaves me less easy to hate. I undo your black belt and ease your pants down below your crotch. It takes some time since your legs are spread apart.

There's a fine layer of nervous moisture over your body. I take a minute to walk around behind you and press up against your hardened damp asscheeks. You flail at the contact and I back off. I smile at the number twenty-four.

Back in front of you, I cup the contents of your jock's pouch in my hand. I squeeze and then start rubbing the area just below the head on the underside of your fat cock. My little trick doesn't work. You don't get any harder, but the sweat keeps pouring down your legs.

I sink to my knees, sliding my tongue along the damp jersey on the way down, my hands still caressing your bulge. I mouth your cock through the reeking ribbed jock. It stings my tongue with strong and subtle flavors. I inhale deeply and close my eyes.

I pull the waistband of your jock down. Your cock falls into my face, then your balls bounce against my beard. They are almost as hairy. I stretch the elastic of the waistband and tuck it behind your balls. I lick them and hold both of them in my mouth, applying pressure until you groan.

Still you aren't getting hard. I laugh out loud and move my open mouth along your cockflesh until I reach the head and slurp it inside. I flick and tease the piss slit, then swallow the whole thing.

All at once you are completely still. Your legs were wavering before, but now you sag in your bondage. You are at the same time completely hard. I choke at the surprise. It feels good to gag on you. My enemy. I tickle you with my mustache and beard and begin to coax you in earnest. I know you don't even realize it, maybe you never will, but I'm raping your cock just as thoroughly as I raped your chunky butt all those nights at home alone in the dark.

Whoever started the idea that sucking a cock is a passive act must have been a deluded man married to a missionary woman.

What could be more aggressive than the hardworking combination of lips, tongue, and throat on a fat piece of manmeat? Of course it's possible to fuck a mouth like you fuck a cunt or an asshole, but that's not what is going to happen here with you. Your stiff dripping meat belongs to me right now, and on some level, as I scrap my teeth lightly on your cockflesh, you know I own it—and you—for this moment. And your outstretched body tells me in a progression of tremors that it has given itself over to the idea finally.

You are the passive one. And if I untied you right now, as your impending orgasm begins to take all your resistant thoughts away, you'd just lie back on the bench until I was done with my business. It's too good now, isn't it? One of my hands grips your asscheek, the middle finger takes its time moving toward your clenching asshole, and the bottom of your jersey pokes me in the eye.

My other hand crawls around blindly in my bag until I find my knife and unsheath it. The metal and stone handle feel so cool compared to your hot pulsating flesh in my throat. I raise the knife blade alongside your thigh.

This is the easiest part. You haven't had a lot of blow jobs like this one, probably never one as good as this. You can't hold it back, even though I've just started to work on you.

I look up into your eyes in time to see that you've just noticed the knife hovering an inch from what is now the center of your universe. The thick vein that runs half the length of your shaft stands up as you unload what I demand from you into my throat in several walnut-flavored deposits. You manage to mash your pubes into my beard, while I graze my fingernail across that naive puckered portal and you surrender the last squirt. I slip the dull edge of the blade against your skin.

You close your eyes so tightly that your temples have crow's feet coming out of them. I cut through the elastic of your jock-strap and it falls at your feet. I slip it into my bag.

And the crowd is hysterical. The game has ended. Old Blue Eyes is singing "New York, New York" over the crappy sound system. The scoreboard strobes its framed fireworks. I have lost sight of you and stand there with my hard-on dribbling. No one will notice it in this carnival. A shirtless young guy with pinstripes crookedly drawn on his face runs by, leading a group of Yankee look-a-likes, all screaming incoherently. People are spilling out of their sections like a foamy tray of over-poured beers.

I just want to get out of here now. Everyone else is frantic with a more evident triumphant glee, as I wipe your imaginary jism off my chapping lips. But I decide to stay until it thins out a bit. I sit back in my seat. I shiver and smile, put my hands in my jacket pockets and see my breath. I wonder if you're in the locker room by now. My dick starts to harden again.

PLAYING GOD

Alana Noël Voth

My story begins in a place called Garden Row Trailer Park, where forty-seven single-wide trailer homes were packed in like sausages on a couple miles of gravel road and random pads of vegetation. I snuck out my bedroom window one night to meet three other guys from the park, one of whom I was in love with: Darry of the fine black hair and sharp elfin ears. Behind the park, near a mucky pond, the four of us smoked cigarettes and stared at the sky while deciding which point of light was "Your Anus."

I leaned against Darry's arm and felt a shiver of heat between us. After a while, watching our cigarette exhaust mingle in midair, I lowered my hand and let my knuckles skim his. "My brother beat up a faggot once," Darry said as I touched him. I exhaled the last bit of cigarette smoke from my lungs, then dropped the cigarette to the ground. "I'm sure my dad has, too," I said.

The stars softened through the water across my eyes. Nobody spoke.

Darry's cigarette smoke curled above me.

After eleven I jogged back to our trailer, Space 39, slipped through the window, and ran into Dad, waiting for me. "That's the last time you do that," he said.

Dad of the corporal punishment, of the ridicule; all this was in his arsenal.

I heard Mom. "Ash, I was worried about you."

"I'm okay." I went looking for a hug, a mother's mercy, scared as always of Dad, but he blocked my way with an arm to my ribs. "Ow," I said.

Dad closed my door with a click of finality, taking Mom with him, and I was swallowed at last by dark and a smell of incense I'd burned. I crawled under the covers, pulled everything over my head then squeezed my eyes shut, thought of Darry, and jerked off in cloistered, breath-bated secret.

My hands were tied behind me. I sat on his couch and asked Nicolas, "Why do you turn every lover into a story?" For a minute, his hand hovered close to my face, and I felt heat from his palm. Felt how my cock hurt, how I hadn't got off, how I was dying here. Nicolas wiped his come from my chin. "Heals you," he said, and I had no idea what he meant, some psycho writerly bullshit, harder still to believe when he got tears in his eyes, and so I shouted, "Untie me right now, I mean it, take this off me!"

I called him names. Among them, *sadist*. Among them, *sick fuck*.

I met Nicolas at an art gallery downtown, not my usual turf. My usual? Bars, not nightclubs, the dingier and darker the better: obscurity, noise. A place where some guy could elbow you in the ribs then snicker like you deserved it. Tia had invited me to the gallery to hear a poet—except I didn't read poems. I liked movies like *300* and *Secretary*, and I liked plants too, except the ones I had were either dead or dying. I found it very hard to keep stuff alive.

About the gallery thing: Tia had said a change of culture would do me good because she was all about getting me over Lance, the mechanic. Four months before, Lance had replaced the starter in my car, and then I'd bought him a beer. Lance was built like David Beckham, tall, lean, and muscled, and he smelled like oily testosterone; sweat in his pits; sweat smearing his neck; grease and sweat on his chest; sweat down the line of his back to his tailbone, where I played before sticking a finger in his ass.

"Pin me," I'd said once, wanting Lance to bear down on my arms with his hot greasy hands while I felt the cold garage floor behind my shoulder blades and tailbone. I wanted to stick my legs in the air while Lance nailed me with merciless precision. I wanted my back to hurt after, bruises, come leaking out my ass for days. Instead, Lance had bent himself over the hood of a car, radio tuned to a rock station, eerie glow coming from the front office where the only light stayed on, and then shown me his sleek muscled ass before he grabbed his cheeks and pulled them apart: hairy asscrack, brown hole, and a heavy set of balls.

"Fuck me," he'd said.

So I'd moved up behind him and then felt him twitch. He'd placed his hands, palms down, on the hood. "Spank me," he'd said.

I'd done so halfheartedly and not exactly knowing why. I'd felt like I was in a movie playing a part I hadn't rehearsed, hadn't even looked at the lines.

"Baby," Tia had said when I told her. "You're the bottom. Come here." She'd hugged me, patting my head.

"I know."

That night at the art gallery downtown, Nicolas, the poet, stood at a podium against a nonsensical backdrop, I guess what you'd call abstract. I'd no idea what the hell it was, the painting behind him; squiggles? Some indication of genius that went over my head. I preferred an elbow to my ribs, a direct hit.

Nicolas had thick Irish-red hair and freckles against a canvas of pale skin, a full feminine mouth; he wasn't on the tall side, and he wore wire-rimmed glasses.

Not my kind of guy, actually.

I drank a martini—vodka, stiff, three olives—and sat next to Tia and listened to Nicolas read. He kept his hands in his pockets. I couldn't tell at the time he'd balled his hands into fists, that he was wound tightly, a hot wire. A white cotton shirt showed his thin, almost angular, arms. Not my kind of fag at all. His voice was clear but soft, so I had to sit forward to hear him....

You asked me to bind you with whatever I found: towels, scarves, long-sleeved shirts, or a jacket torn to rope around your wrists so you could put up a struggle. You swore the way you'd bend and buck and beg beneath me would bring you bliss. You said, Give me a life worth fighting for by making me fight you. I bound you so tight the blood stopped reaching your hands; they went white. There, love, you said, curling your fingers and then straightening them to show me your palms. Kiss me, you said, so I kissed the center of your left hand and then realized how to get rid of my pain by causing you some. I bit your numb fingers. I bit your nipples, the undersides of your arms, the side of your hip, and you shuddered. I heard you gasp and cry, and so I painted your chest with venomous languid spit all the way to your stomach going straight past your cock to your asshole; I rimmed you like I could transfer a current through my tongue to your synapses. Frankenstein was a benevolent monster.

Listening to all this gave me a killer erection. I mean it was killing me. I shifted a few times in my seat, cleared my throat, felt my eyes water, and stared into my martini. Stiff drink.

Tia said in my ear, "Like him, don't you, Ash?" Proud of herself.

As soon as Nicolas finished reading, Tia dragged me to where he sat signing books.

"Ash, Nicolas. Nicolas, this is Ashton, my friend."

"Hi, Ashton. Or do you like Ash?" Nicolas stood behind the table and held out his hand, white with freckles, just like the rest of him. Long fingers.

"Ash is fine." I shook his hand. Good thing I was wearing loose pants. "You like Nicolas or Nick?"

"Nicolas," he said.

"Okay."

"Ash fits you. Sooty eyes."

"Huh?"

"Sooty. You know...so dark blue they look nearly black, and your lashes, black as coal."

"Oh, right." I stared into my drink again, not used to the way this guy talked.

"I meant it as a compliment." Nicolas had sat again behind his books.

"Yeah? Thanks." I looked down on him and felt small.

"Going to mingle," Tia said. "See you." She kissed my cheek and then vanished.

"I enjoyed...you know, hearing you read." Jesus, I felt awkward.

"I've got a Pinot Gris at my place," Nicolas said. "Gift from an editor. Want to join me?"

Option one: *No way do you go to his place. He's too smart for you.*

Option two: *Oh, hell, yes you do.*

"Fine," I said. "If you want." I shrugged then set down my empty martini glass.

"Cool. I hardly ever meet anyone."

"Why's that?"

"Phobic, you know, about social situations." All of a sudden he blushed.

"You're afraid to be social?"

"Yeah, weird."

"I didn't mean it that way." Shit.

Nicolas bent his head to sign another book. He gripped the pen hard enough that his knuckles went white, tendons stood out on his hands.

Nicolas owned a thousand books organized in rows on numerous shelves in every room. I looked around his apartment that night after the reading: cramped maybe, but neat. Nicolas asked if I wanted dinner.

"Oh, yeah, sure."

"Takeout?"

"Okay."

Nicolas picked up the phone and ordered Thai. When the food arrived, Nicolas had to go around digging for change, so I offered to pay, and he blushed and said, "Thanks."

He spent time looking at his food as he ate. He chewed with patient precision. He commented on flavors and textures, and then on the sauce I had on my mouth.

"Oh, shit." We both went for my napkin at the same time.

"Got it," Nicolas said and then wiped my mouth.

After food and a bottle of wine, we sat on the couch, arms at our sides, hands touching.

Nicolas looked at me. I dug my nails into my leg.

"So, um, you been socially phobic awhile?" Fuck; that was the worst question ever.

"Since I can remember."

"Why?" Great, another dumb question.

"Weird, I guess." Nicolas met my eyes. "People make me feel awkward."

"Really?" I was sure I gave him an incredulous look.

"Yeah, if I have to talk to them. I'm good at people watching though. I like to drink stuff in, notice nuances and body language, and catch innuendo. Know what I mean? I like to record information and then try and give it back as art, you know?"

"Huh," I said. Not sure what else to say. "Yeah, pretty cool."

Nicolas smiled. "Art can heal, you know? Writers are a little like medicine men." He lifted the wine bottle and poured more Pinot Gris in his glass. "We're also terrible drunks."

I laughed.

Nicolas finished his wine in one luxurious swoop then set his glass down. "No, seriously. Writers stare into the fucking abyss, Ash. It can drive you a little crazy, making sense from the chaos, art from the pain. It's like playing God," he said.

I didn't know what to say to that either. *Oh, god. He tongue-tied me.* I felt smaller and smaller, and him above me. Nicolas moved in then and took an unbelievable amount of time touching my hair, gazing into the line of my neck, kissing my ear and then my chin before pushing his lips along my eyebrow, leaving a mark on my eyelid. I cupped my cock through my pants, afraid to touch him, not sure what to do. Nicolas kissed me on my mouth. At first, small and tender kissing, then practically violent. He sucked my tongue. I reached for him. Nicolas pulled away, checked me out, like he was reading my face, gauging the temperature.

"You'll have to walk yourself home." He nodded toward a window. "Wet out there."

I sat a moment looking at him, feeling myself blink. Throbbing. It took me a minute to understand. "Okay." I stood from his couch, not liking it but feeling it was exactly the right thing, him shoving me out the door.

Nicolas pushed his mouth to my neck before pulling away again. "See you," he said.

The day after Dad busted me sneaking out he said he was taking Mom to lunch.

"You're not going," he announced.

I shrugged, trying to play cool. Whatever.

Mom said, "David, maybe…"

Dad grabbed me by the arm, pulling me down the hall. "Know why you're not going? Because you run around behind our backs. That's why. Now go to your room."

"Fine," I said.

He shoved me in the general direction.

In my room Dad told me to lie on my bed.

For a second I didn't say anything, confused. He had something with him, I saw now, rope.

"What are you doing?" I was still confused, getting scared.

"Don't fucking mouth off," he said. "Lie on the damn bed like I told you."

I eased around and then lay back, stiff. Mom stood in the doorway. Dad pulled out a few yards of rope. I looked at Mom, who looked at him. "David?"

"Mom?" I said.

Dad tied me to my bedposts using various tricky knots, or so he said.

"Dad, don't."

"Shut up."

"Mom?" I said again.

She shook her head, eyes darting from me to him.

In the doorway, he blocked Mom, and then Dad said, "You can't be trusted, that's why you'll stay here like this." Dad grabbed Mom's elbow. I didn't even catch her eyes as they left.

I lay in a slice of sunlight that came through the curtains and lit me. I became hot and uncomfortable in my jeans and T-shirt and rubbed my wrists raw yanking the ropes. Pissed my pants. Felt my hands go numb. I started crying. Outside my open window I heard a voice. A shadow came through the curtains like the window had given birth to him. He came toward the bed. My cock went hard. Darry never untied the ropes.

Nicolas called three days later and said we should get together again. I said, "When?"

He said, "Now."

"Really?"

"Yeah. Hurry the fuck up."

I got there less than an hour later. We had chicken salad and a Chardonnay. Then I asked Nicolas what he wanted to do.

"Ha!" His eyes glowed. "Drink you with my eyes and then spill you onto the page."

I stared at him.

"What do you call a guy who dates a writer?" He smiled, waiting.

"I don't know. Tell me." I walked right into it.

"Material."

"Whatever the fuck, man." I was a little angry.

"Joking," Nicolas said.

"No, you weren't."

He smiled.

"What happened to the guy in the poem?" Now I waited for him.

Nicolas shook his head. "I'm no good in relationships."

"Everyone's got problems, you know."

"Sure. What's yours?"

"Guess…I want men who don't want me."

"Why?" he said.

"I like…I don't know exactly." I took a breath. "I liked how you cut me off the other night, just shoved me right out the door, kind of mean."

Nicolas put his hand on my leg. He patted my leg. With his hand he began to rub my thigh.

"And I've been thinking about what you read the other night." I swallowed. "You think you'd like to tie me up?"

"Take everything off," he said.

I stood up from the couch. "Serious?" After a moment, I undressed.

"You have a great cock," he said.

"Thanks." I laughed, and cupped my balls.

"Jack off," he said.

"Are you serious?"

"Are you?"

I looked at him, nodded. "Yeah." I curled my hand into a fist around my cock, dripping precum already.

"Nice," Nicolas said. He watched awhile—gave me the shivers.

Nicolas rose from the couch and removed his shirt, showing me his stark freckled chest, so thin I could almost see ribs. He leaned over, bit my nipple, surprising me. It was like an electric current and I gasped. Nicolas smiled against my throbbing flesh. I felt the curve of his mouth against my nipple, then the end of his tongue on my skin. Then teeth again. Without meaning to I leaned toward him, pushing my cock at him, wanting him to touch me. Nicolas pushed me backward onto the couch then used the long sleeves of his shirt to tie my hands behind my back in makeshift cuffs; I felt the drag and squeeze of cloth against my wrists. I didn't fight, but felt sweat pooling in my pits, on my brow. I had one moment of panic. My heart beat harder and I took sharp breaths and then heavier ones, hopeful.

"There, you see, better?" Nicolas held his mouth above mine. "Ash?"

"Yeah." I gasped.

Nicolas kissed me. I raised my hips off the couch, which put pressure on my arms behind me and hurt. Nicolas took off his pants, exposing his long narrow cock bent like a banana, Irish-red pubes, sweet ruddy balls, a toss of freckles on the inside of his thighs, soft stomach, boyish hips. He began to jerk off.

"Fuck," I said and leaned forward.

Nicolas continued to beat off. "Lift your legs," he said.

It was kind of difficult, but I scooted down on the couch so I was able to lean back on my hands and lift my legs spread-eagle in the air. My cock lay rock hard across my stomach. "Shit," I said.

Nicolas positioned himself above me over the couch, crouched in such a way that he was able to fit the head of his cock inside my asshole. He fucked me, pulled out, fucked me some more, then pulled out. "Shit," I said again. My legs shook. My arms ached. I felt like crying. Nicolas pulled his cock out again, wet with precum and ass juice. "Sit up," he said. I did. "Open your mouth." When I'd done that, Nicolas yanked off a fat ribbon of spunk, which hit me in my chin.

"You'll make a beautiful story," he said. I shouted at him, called him terrible names. Nicolas untied the ropes.

THE HARNESS

Doug Harrison

The San Francisco morning fog was burning off as I sauntered along Polk Street, a scene I know well. I could easily be a guide for visiting perverts hankering to explore the seedy stores displaying girlie magazines, lascivious lingerie, and multicolored dildos from small to huge behind their unwashed, scratched windows. My specialty, however, is an in-depth knowledge of establishments with more than a token gay presence of a few sticky magazines containing photos of overendowed muscle builders. I'm a connoisseur of stores that speak directly to the city's serious gay population with glossy hard core sealed in cellophane; locked display cases of cock rings, ball stretchers, and tit clamps; and rows of clapboard booths for viewing gay porn with waist-high, cock-sized openings in their stained walls.

But that day, after wandering over to Hayes Street, past a pizza parlor and pawnshop, I came to a small unfamiliar shop fronting a freshly swept sidewalk, with sparkling windows. My eyes danced among shiny black leather chaps, pants, jackets, vests, caps, and polished boots shimmering in an array of pressed 501s, denim work shirts, and tank tops. Soft chimes announced my entrance with the first three notes of "One Fine Day" from *Madame Butterfly*.

A rail-thin man with a salt-and-pepper beard and thinning crew cut ambled my way as I scanned the shop. He was dressed in tight leather pants and a blue work shirt. He looked me over and smiled.

"Welcome," he said, and extended his hand. We shook as I returned his grin, but his frail, bony hand belied his attempt to appear vigorous.

"Nice store," I offered.

"My partner's dream," he replied, and dropped his head. He looked up abruptly. "Interested in anything in particular?"

I hesitated as I scanned the racks and cases. "Something in leather."

He nodded, smiled, and followed my glance to a rack of harnesses. We approached the assortment of minimal, but essential uniforms for Tops and bottoms, Daddies and boys, or Masters and slaves.

A spotlit harness hanging from hooks on the wall above the display caught my attention. My jaw dropped.

It was a Top's harness. A harness that reflected the authority and supplemented the respect due its owner. Not a bottom's harness with thin straps that crisscross shoulders and chest, but a full body harness with two-inch-wide heavy leather straps, V-shaped over the shoulders, riveted in front and back to thick metallic semicircular rings, and adjusted with one-inch by two-inch heavy metal buckles. The buckle thongs were kept in place with matching metal grommets set into the leather, unlike the punched holes of cheap harnesses. Two matching straps and buckles joined the front and rear rings by passing around the torso just below the nipples.

My cock twitched as I admired this masterpiece of leather and metal workmanship.

A leather strap, *V*-shaped at the top, traveled from the metallic ring and was riveted to a leather triangle that covered the crotch area. The triangle was secured in place by straps and buckles that passed around the waist and also matched the shoulder straps. A detachable pouch with a dozen or so symmetrical, gleaming studs was fastened to the triangle by three snaps. Two adjustable leather straps about one-half-inch wide went from the bottom of the triangle to the waistband. *Most unusual, just like a jockstrap.* I could imagine the leather biting into the juncture between my thighs and cheeks, perhaps tugging on a hair or two as I tightened the straps to frame my ass. My cock now throbbed.

Finally, I reveled at the four gleaming chains that went from codpiece and waistband, front and back, to the large torso rings, front and back. A slow breath out was overtaken by my gasp. My face flushed as my dick pushed against the thin fabric of my jeans; the bulge was not to be denied.

The salesman's gaze traveled from my face to my crotch and returned to my eyes.

"Would you like to try it on?"

I nodded. He fetched a long wooden pole with a metal hook, lowered the harness, and stood facing me. "My name's Ned," he said.

"Brad. Glad to meet you."

We again shook hands as he offered the harness to me, not in a tangle of fists, arms, and leather, but with a fluid motion. We held on to each other and the harness, prolonging the exchange, and swimming in a bittersweet emotion I sensed but could not fathom.

I entered the dressing room, mirrored on three sides, and the knee-to-chest-high door swung shut behind me. Ned smiled from across the aisle. "Let me know if you need any help."

"Sure enough." I grinned back. He retreated to the rear of the store.

I undressed, and my cock sprang forth. The side mirrors were angled at forty-five degrees, so I could examine my butt full view. *Not bad for an old fart.* I removed the codpiece, loosened the shoulder, waist, and side straps, slithered into the harness, and pushed and tugged my dick and balls through the opening in the front piece. *This feels great, and I haven't even tightened anything.* I leisurely rotated a full turn, not simply to inspect the total package, but to feel the harness grasping me. I stopped, closed my eyes, and sank into my self-imposed bondage. *Ironic, the Top imposes bondage upon himself to accentuate his authority.* I adjusted the shoulder straps and waistband, but the torso buckles proved elusive. *Damn!* I fiddled with them.

"How's it going in there?" Ned asked.

"Er...uh..." I stammered.

"So, you do need help," he offered over the top of the door. *How long's he been watching me?*

"Yes, please," I said.

" 'Please' is not necessary," he said as he stepped into my booth and looked at my boner. "Nice, very, very nice." He adjusted the torso buckles, stepping close enough that the tip of my dick grazed his crotch.

"I'll let you adjust the leg straps," he said.

As I tightened them, he asked, "Feel good?"

"You know damn well it does!" *Encased in thick, tight leather straps, but totally free.* I put my hands on my hips and stared at Ned.

"You'll never get the pouch on over that monster dick," he said.

"I know. I'll have to take for granted that it fits."

"Perhaps not," he offered. He sank to his knees and looked up. "Okay?" he asked as his warm breath floated over my dick.

A slight pause. "Yeah, boy," I said.

Then I grabbed his head with both hands and shoved my dick into his mouth. He didn't gag.

I pumped. He didn't retch.

I relaxed, pulled my cock partway out, and stroked his head. "Good boy," I whispered.

He looked up. Tears crept down his cheeks. He reached up and fondled my nipples.

"Oh, yeah," I gasped. "You can't hurt them. Try, boy, try."

Ned dug his fingernails in and yanked as his tongue slid back and forth along my shaft.

"Fuck, yes. Someone's trained you well, boy."

Ned tongued my piss slit and stared into the distance. His tears were very real. "Yes, Sir, someone has. Come in me, Sir."

My eyebrows arched.

"Please, Sir, please." I thought his fingernails would meet through the rough skin of my nipples.

I nodded.

Ned buried his head in my crotch. I felt his tears through my pubic hair. I teetered at the edge of orgasm. He grabbed the ass straps of the harness and the leather tightened against my perineum.

I exploded. I spurted. I spasmed.

I emptied myself into him.

I pushed my palms against the walls to steady myself as my convulsions subsided.

I softened as he laved the end of my dick with his tongue

and leaned back on his haunches. He brushed the tears from
his cheeks, dropped his head, and looked up abruptly. "Thank
you," he sighed.

"Thank you," I answered between gulps of air.

"No, thank you very much, more than you'll ever know."

I ran my hand over his head.

"I'll help you get out of the harness."

We began to undress me. "They don't make harnesses like
this anymore," I said. "It's very old, isn't it?"

"Yes. It's vintage San Francisco," Ned answered. "Shall I put
it in a bag for you?"

"Please." I didn't ask the price.

Ned left the booth, and I dressed and wandered over to the
solitary counter. He watched me approach, and a smile crossed
his lips. He slid a large, shiny black bag toward me.

"How much," I asked as I tugged my wallet from my
pocket.

"Nothing," he whispered.

"I...I...I can't do that," I stammered.

Ned reached across the counter and rested his index finger
on my lips. "It belonged to my partner," he said. "I want you to
have it. I want this harness to have a good home. You deserve
each other. I can tell."

Again we stared at each other. It was my turn to cry. Ned
walked around the counter and held me. We both sobbed. He
thrust the bag into my arms and walked me to the door.

"Till we meet again," he said.

"Again," I answered, as the door closed behind me.

I blinked into the sunlight. I stepped right, turned left, and
finally continued in my original direction. I reached Civic Center,
watched as healthy straight folks—mothers with their babies,
kids on bikes and roller skates, and teenagers necking—acted

out their lives. A few gay couples trundled past.

My car and a possible parking ticket beckoned many blocks away. I retraced my steps, but on the opposite side of the street. I slowed and stopped when I came to the leather store. I looked through the traffic, and started to wave and blow a kiss.

The store was closed.

NORCEUIL'S GARDEN

Andrew Warburton

The door opened as I approached and a handsome, middle-aged man in pin-striped trousers and a black tailcoat ushered me inside. The checked marble slabs sparkled beneath his feet, as did the polished tips of his shoes, and from the bright chandelier above our heads, thousands of tiny lights exploded, covering the banisters, the walls, and the floor. Beside the stand where the butler draped my coat, I caught my reflection in a wall-length mirror: I could see the fine white hairs at my temples, the sagging skin around my neck, and something like regret rose insidiously in my chest.

The butler coughed gently. "If you'd like to follow me into the garden, sir."

We walked through the hall and out through a pair of doors into a courtyard, which opened onto a garden. That morning, when I received the invitation from Norceuil, I knew to expect something rich and sumptuous, surpassing my expectations—but this was something else entirely. Row upon row of trees stretched endlessly into darkness, with giant cobwebs hanging like nets between the branches. I could hear the breeze whispering in the leaves, and somewhere not too far away, the sound of people laughing and moaning. As I made my way toward them, I had to slash the cobwebs with my hands and watch the tiny spiders scuttle away.

The wood opened up then and I found myself in a clearing where the air itself seemed to shimmer with silver. The moon was not quite full but it shone brightly, making everything glitter, from the smallest blade of grass to the heaviest branch spangled with leaves. A group of elderly men were standing on the other side of the clearing. They were dressed in smart suits and carried cocktail glasses with misted sides. I could see the ice sparkling in the liquid, which they sipped with their wrinkled lips, and as I walked across the grass toward them, a waiter glided past me bearing a tray on which glass after glass was lined up. He handed one to me and quickly glided away.

The men didn't turn as I approached. They were transfixed by something on the nearest tree trunk. Some of them were laughing; others were wincing, covering their eyes. *What on earth are they looking at?* I thought, as I stood on the tips of my toes.

What I saw surprised me. A young man was strapped to the tree, totally naked but for thick leather bonds that pulled his arms and legs agonizingly far apart. He was peering through a mop of blond hair at a group of three or four gentlemen who were poking and prodding his muscular thighs and calves. "Stop it, stop it," he groaned, shaking at his bonds, but the old men ignored him and continued manhandling his cock.

"What's going on here?" I said to the man beside me, who was watching it all through a monocle.

"Didn't you get the invite? *Rare specimens,* it said, *in the*

first flush of youth. And that's exactly what Norceuil's got!"
The man laughed, turning to the others. "Gentlemen, we have a
latecomer!"

All at once the crowd turned to face me. I could see the glee
in their eyes, the flush of arousal in their cheeks.

"Come, come!" said a craggy-faced old man, ushering me
toward the tree. "Taste of the fruits of paradise! 'Tis manna for
the likes of us!"

I stopped at the foot of the tree and looked up at the young
man who was spread before me in all his glory. His cock was
swollen and red, his balls knotted at the base. He looked at
me with pleading eyes, as if to say, *Save me, sir, from these
barbarians!*

"Quickly," said the old man, who still had hold of my arm.
"Don't keep us waiting. There're plenty of us here and we'd all
like a go with him!"

The young man's face fell as I reached up and took his enormous, bloated cock in my hands. I brought it to my lips. The
crowd cheered and the young man groaned as I slid the cock
across my tongue. *Gosh,* I thought, *how long has it been since
I've taken a cock in my mouth and sucked this greedily?*

The young man struggled like a madman, shouting till he
was red in the face. His cock grew harder all the time and his
balls screwed up tight. Reaching up, I flicked them and listened
to the cry of pain.

"He's coming!" someone shouted. "Look at him! He's coming
in an old man's mouth!"

I looked up, and for a moment, between slurps, I caught
his eye, and there was nothing but hatred there—and shame.
Grasping hold of his cock, I sucked ferociously. His chest rose
and fell, faster and faster, and he hurled abuse at me, telling
me he'd find me and kill me if I didn't stop what I was doing. I

merely took the end, licked it before his very eyes and resumed the sucking. He fell silent then. His whole body tensed. The way his cock bucked and bounced on my tongue, it was as if it had become a living thing, quite separate from the rest of him, and I had to suck harder just to keep it in place.

All of a sudden, the tension went out from the shaft, into the head. Again and again it sprayed on my tongue, and that bitterness I knew so well washed through me, and I swallowed it down. His cock went limp and I carried on sucking; now his whole body fell limp against the bark, and his legs brushed against me, his skin wet and burning.

I stepped back from the tree and wiped the saliva from my mouth. The men around me cheered and slapped my back. The young man put his head to the side and shut his eyes. His chest was heaving. I reached up and pinched his ass. He didn't stir. I could see the delicate black lashes around his eyes, the pale skin. I tweaked his nipples, but still he didn't move. He was exhausted, poor thing, the strength drained out of him: I could taste it on my tongue.

The trees stood in rows that seemed to go on forever, masses of leaves falling around them like great shaggy manes. The wood was less dense now, but traces of silver still floated between the branches. The men led me through the silent aisles, discussing the subjects that were dear to their hearts: politics, medicine, and law. I found I had nothing interesting to say and fell silent. I kept thinking of that young man's cock, the look of fury in his eyes as the cum sprayed out of him. I wanted to relive it again and again.

Through the trees I saw the edge of a white tent. Tiny blue stars on the walls kept fading in and out, and there were groups of old men inside, drinking and laughing merrily. I took a crystal flute from a handsome waiter and sipped the bubbly, fruity wine.

A bell rang then and a hush fell around the room. As if from nowhere, Norceuil appeared. He was standing on a platform at the front of the tent, looking every inch the fop. I'd always found Norceuil rather fetching. He was handsome in a fine-boned, arty sort of way, and gifted with a keen intelligence that often left me feeling inadequate. With a gentle cough, he introduced himself to the crowd: "Gentleman, I hope you're enjoying yourselves. We've spared no expense to bring you the finest wines, the finest meats, the finest *youths*. I want you to relax and be merry. We have all night!"

The tent exploded with cheers.

Norceuil smiled, making a quietening gesture with his hands, "Hush, gentlemen, hush. That only leaves me to introduce dessert!"

To the merriment of the men, two waiters carrying an enormous tray appeared at the side of the stage. A young man was tied to the four corners of the tray in such a way that his ass was pushed out and up in the air—and what a full, ripe ass it was! The man had a swimmer's body, with broad shoulders and thighs, and arms so muscular they veritably rippled. I watched now as the waiters placed the tray at Norceuil's feet.

"Now, now, gentlemen," he said, hushing the room, "You may recognize this boy. That's right, gentleman. It's the vice president's son! Ivy League Football Rookie of the Year! We promised you men in the first flush of youth—rare specimens, we said, and that's exactly what we've brought you. Kidnapped from his father's mansion, no less. Take him! He's all yours! His ass and his mouth! Do with him what you will!"

With a flourish, Norceuil backed away to watch the proceedings from the side of the stage. The men cheered, pressing closer.

Holding my glass safely against my chest, I inched forward.

There were so many of the men pressed around the young man I had to stand on the tips of my toes and peer over their shoulders just to get a look. What I saw made it all worthwhile and caused my cock to swell immediately. The boy was sobbing, pressing his face against the tray, and the men were all over him, running their hands over his ass and his long muscular thighs, or slipping their fingers around his heavy balls and giving them a good squeeze. One had stuck his thumb in the boy's ass and was rigorously moving it in and out, fascinated by the motion. Another had prized the boy's lips apart and was pushing the head of his cock against the boy's teeth, which stubbornly refused to open.

For a moment I felt a wave of sympathy for this bright young star from his Ivy League university. He was innocent, after all, and these men were beasts—fat, egotistical monsters. I looked at them now and felt slightly queasy. How many chins did they have between them? And those stomachs—like pot-bellied pigs! As they bent over the boy to reach for some extremity or limb, their stomachs pressed his tender flesh, and no matter how small he tried to make himself, he couldn't escape their bulging fat.

One of the men, a renowned lawyer from Boston, unzipped his fly and let his trousers and pants fall down around his ankles. He positioned himself at the boy's ass and held his flaccid penis in his hands. The other men watched eagerly. It didn't seem to have occurred to the lawyer that the athlete was as tight as a drum, because what he did next had me in stitches of laughter. He put his cock against the boy's hole and tried to squeeze the head inside, but because it was so soft it just kept slipping out, wiping precum over the boy's ass.

The boy looked terrified, as if he'd been stabbed. He bucked his legs and waved his ass in the air, trying to escape his restraints, trying to get away from the lawyer's cock.

The lawyer's face reddened. He was evidently frustrated now, which merely seemed to make him more determined. He grasped hold of the boy's hips and thrust his cock towards the boy's ass. Again his cock slipped everywhere. The boy tried desperately to move his ass away, but the lawyer had hold of him now and wasn't letting go. Eventually the lawyer's cock began to harden. He shoved it up to the hilt in the boy's ass and started rocking backward and forward on his heels, a look of intense satisfaction on his face. It was just at this moment, as the boy groaned and threw back his head, that another gentleman decided to shove his cock in the boy's mouth. He slid it in as far as it would go, till the boy's lips were buried in the thick hairs around his balls. The man pulled his cock out and thrust it in again. The boy spluttered, his eyes widened and saliva leaked from the corners of his mouth.

"I'm coming," said the lawyer in a deep, gravelly voice as he continued to slide in and out. "I'm coming inside you, stud!"

The gentleman at the other end (whose balls were squashed against the young man's lips) yelled, "Me too, kiddo! Get ready!"

The lawyer's eyes rolled back in his head. He tightened his grip around the boy's waist and slammed his hips into the boy's ass. Convulsions ran through his entire body. He threw himself forward across the boy's back and kissed him everywhere, squeezing his cock. The other gentleman groaned and his cock exploded against the boy's face. The boy grimaced as cum dripped the length of his nose onto his lips.

Norceuil sprang forward to the edge of the stage. He smiled broadly, clapping his hands above his head. "Good show! A roasting from both ends!"

The crowd watched with some admiration as the two men zipped up their trousers and walked away from the stage.

"My fellow men," said Norceuil, "I wish you a stupendous

evening. Please feel free to explore, and do sample whatever takes your fancy."

To the cheers of the audience, he bowed and dismounted from the stage.

Now the amusements were over, I walked to the door and looked out. The sight that confronted me was very different from the one I'd left upon entering the tent. Everywhere I looked young men were strapped to the trees—each one a beauty to behold, with ripe, muscular bodies, enormous cocks, and classically handsome features. The best thing of all was the dismay on their faces. Not only did they look terrified, but also deeply ashamed. As I moved through the glistening trees, I saw men sucking on the young men's cocks, pinching their thighs and ample backsides, or picking things up off the forest floor and sticking them into every orifice they could find. The crying and shouting that went up from the boys formed a terrible din, so earth-shatteringly noisy one could almost believe that Hell had opened in this very wood!

Taking a flute from a passing waiter, I sipped the bubbly wine. Already it had gone to my head, filling me with the strange sensation of floating. As I swam happily between the trees, I thought nothing of slapping a cock here, tugging one there, or slipping my hands around a slim boy's waist and licking the end of his cock. But soon I found that I was quite, quite lost, with no idea which direction to take.

"Uncle," said a deep voice behind me.

I turned around. Immediately I recognized the long, Roman nose, the full luscious lips. It was my nephew, Taylor! Totally naked like the others, he was tied to an oak tree on my right hand side, his legs pulled wide apart.

I smiled casually. What a sight for sore eyes! "Taylor," I said warmly, stretching my hand toward him before realizing he had no way of shaking it. "Oh, I'm sorry, I forgot." Instead I shook his cock.

"Uncle!"

"I'm sorry. You can't shake my hand, you see. I thought I was doing you a favor."

"Uncle, you have to get me out of here! They kidnapped me."

I feigned surprise. "No! Really?"

"Yes! You've got to help me!"

"Taylor, I'm not sure I can do that. Even if I untied you, there's no way we could escape together. There are men everywhere and we'd be seen."

"Uncle, I don't care. You have to get me down. You could hide me somewhere in the bushes and come back for me."

"Hush, Taylor, hush, you're getting yourself excited."

"Uncle, what are you talking about! You've got to help me!"

I looked up at his flushed cheeks and the ruffled blond hair on his head. He looked so innocent, so imploring, I almost did as he said. But then my hand went up, almost involuntarily and grabbed hold of his cock.

"Uncle! What are you doing?"

I started jacking him off, at first slowly but gradually getting faster and faster. "Stop it, Uncle! Please! What are you doing?" He struggled and kicked at his bonds, but they were too cleverly knotted around him.

"You definitely take after your uncle in this department," I chortled, amazed by the length and width of his cock. His eyes were frantic as I moved the foreskin back and forth across the head. With the other hand I reached up to pinch his pale pink nipples, then, still chortling to myself quietly, I took his balls in my palm and jiggled them up and down.

"Uncle, please," he said in a serious voice, but I carried on pumping his cock, now gently, now with abandon. His face was beginning to redden now and every so often he would lick his lips and his eyes would roll around in their sockets. He was about to come. "Uncle, please, I don't want to come. Don't let me. Stop!"

But it was too late. A massive jolt ran through his cock and jet after jet of cum flew with great momentum from the tip. His whole body went into spasms and he groaned deep within his chest. I pumped his cock till the last drop of cum had dripped from the end then I took a step back and looked up.

He looked like he was sleeping, his handsome face on one side.

"Good-bye, Taylor. I enjoyed that very much."

I started backing out between the trees.

"Wait," he said quietly. "Uncle, you have to help me."

I smiled softly. "Anytime, Taylor. Just give me a call. I'm good, aren't I? If you'd like it to happen again, just call."

As I walked away, his cries began to echo louder and louder through the wood. Looking down, I saw his cum on my hands. Grimacing, I wiped it in the grass.

The horizon was a rich, dark blue by the time I made it back to the tent. Stars still twinkled in the middle of the sky, but lower down they'd all been wiped out.

I sat down on a large rock and looked deep into the trees. The young men's cries still rippled through the wood, but they were fainter now, more pathetic—hardly distinguishable from the calls of the awakening birds.

"What a night," said an old fellow next to me, his eyes bleary with drink.

"Yes," I murmured. "Quite a night."

The man chuckled. "And weren't they convincing? Norceuil got it just right. All paid actors, of course…College *is* expensive these days…"

"Yes," I murmured, trying to fully grasp what he had said. "But my nephew, Taylor…?"

"Oh, you know Taylor? He's been making very good use of his holiday break, I can tell you!"

I sat on, musing on all I'd seen and heard. On the outskirts of the clearing, the leaves had begun to catch the first rays of morning. I plucked one from the forest floor and held it up to the sky. Veins ran through the crisp brown skin like finely threaded gold. I dropped it and watched it glide peacefully to the ground. A line of light was creeping across the forest floor. It traveled up my ankle and warmed my skin, and for an instant it seemed as if the trees were burning. Then the sun rose from the treetops and rays of yellow light burst through the air. "And now it's over," I said.

The man nodded. I stood up and slowly made my way back toward the house.

THE MAN WHO TIED HIMSELF UP

Simon Sheppard

(based on a true story)

There was a man lived in our town, and Arthur was his name. Oh, Arthur had his kinks of course, just like any of us does. He liked to eat ass, he liked to be spanked, and sometimes, if he was in a very, very good mood, he liked to drink other men's pee.

But mostly, Arthur liked to get tied up.

Because he was a most attractive young man, Arthur generally had no trouble finding other attractive young men to do the tying up. He would follow them home, take off all his clothes—a process that always left Arthur's extraordinarily large penis stiff and dripping-wet—and allow whoever it was to tie him down to their bed with whatever clothesline came to hand. But this left poor, well-hung Arthur somewhat dissatisfied.

So he began to seek out less attractive, less young men— fellows who presumably knew more about what they were doing—to tie him up instead. This was a good decision. Not only were these men less self-absorbed and more knowledgeable, many of them were well heeled enough to have amassed sizable collections of pricey bondage gear. Suspension harnesses, black leather bondage mitts, tight-fitting cowhide hoods...all sorts of swell new gimcracks now played a part in Arthur's perverted little sessions.

Still, no matter how skilled and solicitous his temporary masters were, there was always *something* unsatisfactory. One man talked too much, another maintained stony silence. There were tops who left him feeling too loosely restrained, others who stretched Arthur's naked body out to the point of discomfort.

So Arthur began to tie himself up.

Ah, that was more like it. Now he was sure to get what he wanted, with none of those disappointments that occurred when other men were involved.

Arthur started slow. In the beginning, he would strip down and, a length of soft rope at his side, lie down on his bed and jack off. When his big, beautifully formed cock was fully hard, he would pick up the rope and loop it around the base of his cock and balls. Tightening the loop would cause the blood to be trapped in his dickshaft, making it bulge even more and turn a pleasant, darkish shade, a pink tinged with purple. He would tie the rope off with a square knot—left over right, right over left—and lie back to look at his handiwork. Simple as the arrangement was, it gave him a great deal of pleasure, and when he spit in his hand and caressed his hard shaft, it was an excellent feeling indeed.

Soon, Arthur's dick-tying sessions became more elaborate. He would use a longer piece of rope to bind his balls, stretching them out just right, then winding coils of clothesline around the base of his sac till his nuts were bulging beneath slick and shiny skin. If he were feeling even more ambitious, he would tie his shaft up, too, winding rope around his hard prick until only the tip of his dick showed, its distended piss slit glimmering with pooled precum.

Sometimes he would slap around his tied-up package, stopping just at the point when pleasure was about to become pain, and then he'd rapidly pull the ropes off, exposing a bobbling, hard cock just begging to be brought to climax.

This all went so satisfactorily that Arthur soon embarked on more elaborate scenarios. At first, he would take a long piece of rope and wind it around both of his graceful, hairy ankles, then loop it crosswise between his legs and tie it off, leaving his ankles firmly restrained in rope cuffs. Just the process of doing so made him intensely excited, and he would struggle against his restraints as he beat his tied-up dick off to a frothy resolution. He began to take pictures of himself, at first by triggering the timer on his 7-megapixel Olympus, then by setting up his video camera and flat-panel TV to provide a real-time feed, instant bondage porn he could watch as he masturbated. Bondage porn starring himself.

He then proceeded to experiment with more restrictive play. As the video camera winked, he tied his bound-together feet to the footboard of his bed, then added a rope that secured his left arm to the headboard. It all looked quite nice on-screen, but he yearned for even more. So he went online and ordered sets of wrist and ankle restraints from a well-known purveyor of S/M accoutrements.

When the much-anticipated package arrived, Arthur immediately opened it, took off all his clothes, and tightly cinched down the ankle restraints. Just walking around his house wearing leather cuffs gave him a hard-on that wouldn't quit, so he lay down, clipped the restraints together, and tied them to the footboard of his bed. He came almost immediately.

In the days that followed, he proceeded to choreograph ever more elaborate scenes. At first, he put on one of the wrist restraints, roping it to the headboard after his ankles were securely bound. Then he added the second one, managing to maneuver all four limbs into a spread-eagle position, afterward undoing the bondage with his teeth. When he was feeling particularly festive, he would add tit clamps and a gag. He briefly considered a blindfold, but that would have meant being unable to watch himself on the video hookup as he squirmed in ostensible powerlessness. He left his eyes unblocked.

Some of the men who had tied him up in the past (mostly those to whom he hadn't displayed obvious disappointment) would occasionally get in touch with him, wanting to play again. But Arthur had found a superior bondage top: himself. There was really no reason to accept second-best. All the offers were politely refused.

In his quest for bigger and better thrills, Arthur took his show on the road. At first, the changes of scene were minor. He built a bondage board in his basement, for instance, and took great delight in enmeshing his own squat-but-muscular body in increasingly elaborate webs of rope and chain. With a tripod and his camera's time-lapse setting, documenting the dungeonesque scenes was a snap. But even that paled after a while; as lovely as his tumescent self-portraits undoubtedly were, Arthur longed for the aesthetic next step, something to accurately document how beautiful his bound-up body actually was.

Arthur had grown up in a small town in the Mojave. The place had been something of a pit, but he had always loved the sight of the surrounding desert, especially the sand dunes at sunrise. He decided to incorporate that beauty in his pornographic self-portraiture.

One Saturday afternoon he drove back to his hometown, taking care not to stop long enough to be spotted by anyone he knew, especially his parents. He drove out past the gas station his father ran, out to the towering sand dunes. He put up a freestanding tent, set his alarm clock for just before dawn, and crawled into his sleeping bag.

When he awoke in the dark, it was chilly; the high desert got cold at night. But the full moon was still above the horizon, and Arthur lost no time striking the tent and stripping down. He left his clothes and cell phone in the car, and, carrying his camera, tripod, and a bag of bondage gear, climbed up a nearby dune, oddly horny from shivering naked in the near-dawn. Though he was only about a half mile from town, he figured the chance of being glimpsed at such an early hour was minimal. Still, the vague possibility added a piquant edge to the proceedings.

He sank the legs of the tripod into the sand and set the camera at an angle that would catch the image of him lying on the sand, the red glow of dawn illuminating both timeless sands and straining flesh. Fiddling for a moment, he set the camera on time-exposure so it would take a new picture every sixty seconds.

Arthur had recently purchased two pairs of shiny steel hand-cuffs, hoping that his photographs would capture the glint of early-morning sunlight on metal. Since the sunrise would take a goodly while, he fastened a cock ring around the base of his penis and balls; he was hard as a rock now, but why take any chances? And rather than rope up his dick, he spread baby oil on the arc of hard flesh—the movie director in him hoped his cock would gleam with the morning sunlight, too.

Making certain the handcuff keys were attached to his car keys, so they wouldn't get lost, he sat down on the side of the rather steep dune. The shots would not only capture the image of his body, but a vista of the desert beyond. It would, he hoped, look breathtaking. But then, Arthur designed window displays for pricey clothing stores. He knew about breathtaking.

Leaning over, he fastened one pair of cuffs around his ankles; the sound of the metal ratcheting down cut excitingly through the desert silence. Then he painstakingly cuffed his wrists together, his right hand keeping a tight grip on the keys. He knew from numerous practice sessions that, by gripping the key between his teeth and maneuvering just so, he'd be able to undo the lock.

The camera had been snapping pictures all along, making a nostalgic electronic click that sounded just like the shutter of a film camera. And the sun hovered just below the horizon now, turning the east red. It was all perfect, perfectly arranged. Except for the sand up the crack of his ass; he hadn't anticipated that, but he could wash the grit off later. Arthur lay back on the dune, twisting himself so the shine of cuffs around his ankles would be caught by the lens. He raised his arms above his head and stretched his muscular torso upward. His gleaming cock pointed toward the heavens.

As minutes passed, each one demarcated by a *click*, Arthur began to trance out, the way he often did in bondage scenes. It was a kind of sexual excitement that verged on the narcotic, the sort of thrill he found nowhere else. And now there would be a record, a beautiful portfolio of his bondage in the Mojave Desert.

It began as a faint, distant whistle. But soon enough, the sound of wind became a *whoosh*. The sand was getting whipped up, blowing everywhere. Fuck, the camera! Oh, well, it couldn't be helped. Arthur shut his eyes tight, hoping that the sandstorm would calm down soon. But for one careless moment, he relaxed his lids, and sand got in his eyes. He brought his hands to his face to protect himself, and as he did, threw himself off balance. Arthur began rolling down the dune. He threw his bound-together hands out in an effort to break his fall, and as he did, Arthur let go of the keys.

He came to rest near the base of the dune, not far from his car. But great pinkish-tan avalanches of sand were still sheeting down the dunes, and the keys were nowhere to be seen. Trying to crawl back up the hill in the wind took Herculean effort, but he gave it a shot, rooting around in the sand for the lost key ring.

No dice.

The wind had died down, but he was well and truly fucked. Oh, well, he might not be able to get dressed, he might feel foolish, but he could go back to the car and phone someone to rescue him, call one of the ex-boyfriends whose numbers were programmed into his phone. It might be early, but he knew that at least a couple of them were likely to have been up all night.

Cautiously, he rolled himself away from the dune, sand covering his sticky hard-on. He got to the car, struggled to his knees, and grabbed the door handle.

Fuck. Fuck fuck fuck. For no reason at all, he had unthinkingly locked himself out of his car.

And that was how Arthur came to be hopping and hobbling down a desert road in the pale, cool morning. For a while, his big dick remained hard, bobbing ahead of the rest of his naked body. He remembered the cock ring, unsnapped it, and his penis soon deflated, but the occasional jackrabbit couldn't have cared one way or the other.

The heat of the day was just beginning to hit when Arthur, exhausted, reached the tumbleweed-strewn edge of his hometown. Out in front of the Arco, his father was setting out the rack of motor oil.

Demurely, Arthur lowered his cuffed-together hands till they almost hid his dick.

"Hello, Dad," he said.

DON'T THROW ME INTO THAT BRIAR PATCH!

(TIED TO THE RAILROAD TRACKS OF LOVE: HOW I ONCE SEDUCED MYSELF INTO KNOTS NO SAILOR EVER KNEW)

Jack Fritscher

'm not interested," he says, "in the casual trick who wants to get tied up for three hours, fucked, and then be untied and let go. I do bondage best from referrals. I want to know the man really likes to be tied up in a prolonged scene. The first bondage training session should last a minimum of thirty-six hours. After all, this is not a game. Bondage is a lifestyle. A day and a half restrained in rope, chains, or mummification is not a major commitment. A full scene should last ten days."

He's real. He's totally real, sitting here in his Los Angeles apartment. He's got my attention. Now if he can only hold my interest. "You mean then," I say, "some guys come to you here in L.A. and spend their entire vacation in bondage?"

"That kind of major scene is not uncommon, but the shorter thirty-six-hour trip is a valid training period. In and out of bondage. Say four hours of rigid, total, immobile bondage, broken with short extreme periods of even more intense and tighter bondage. Good bondage style alternates the basic immobile states with the heavier intense state, and then adds in periods of light restraint with leg irons, wrist cuffs, and a collar. Even some duties to perform. Bondage reinforces the master-slave relativity. When a man is immobile for eight hours, he learns to know his place. Restraining his body binds his mind, locks him into a space of servitude."

He knots and unknots a long length of rope grayed from much use. His knotting motion is not nervous. He fondles the rope casually, expertly in his big hands. He stands six feet and weighs well over two hundred. He is blond and good-looking with one tattoo on his muscular right forearm. He is a beefed up, matured version of the surfer he once was.

"During a thirty-six-hour scene," he says, "the bondage master must exercise enough sensitivity to know what light, to medium, to severe restraint his bondage slave can handle."

"You're like a professor of bondage."

"I'm more like a tour guide."

"Of rope tricks."

"Of the windmills of your mind."

I uncross my legs and cross them again. "Some guys," I say, "have some idea how much bondage they can take; maybe restraint as simple as handcuffs; as medium as a spread-eagle stretch, ankles and wrists, standing up or lying down; as severe as a total body-harness suspension, hooded, blindfolded, gagged, and covered with a gas mask."

He looks at me. "Some men prefer total mummification." He opens a drawer. "Wrapped completely in Ace bandages or leather or rubber. Tied into a straightjacket, then rolled into wet sheets, and strapped down with leather belts. Tied into a ball, hooded, dropped in a canvas sack, nailed into a wooden crate, buried in a ventilated hole in the cellar."

I touch my crotch. "Is this supposed to be making me hard?"

"That's one of the seductions of bondage. A man has some idea of how far under he'd like to go; and as I take him there, he finds that he wants to go farther, heavier, than he first believed."

"Bondage is addictive?"

"What fetish isn't addictive? Bondage is a kind of wonderful downer. A relaxant from the world's fast pace. Bondage is by its nature meditative. Once a guy acquires a taste for restraint, he automatically moves into a higher level of sensual sophistication."

"Do you mind if I hit my popper?"

"Why not? If a guy needs a joint to calm down on arrival or to swallow something before he arrives, that's his business. Once I put the first restraint on him, the slave has no movement he can call his own. As his bondage master, I control what goes into his body. I'm no prohibitionist, but I don't use drugs. I need to be clear enough to monitor my immobile slave's condition."

"What if a guy needs poppers for pain?"

"That's a variation on a theme. Like adding a suffocation trip into the bondage, putting his breathing into bondage in a Gas Mask Scene. I can fill the rubber gas mask tube with whatever I want my slave to breathe or re-breathe. Popper. Cigar smoke."

"Shit!"

"If it's on the menu."

"What if a guy chickens out because he's being coiled and wrapped and bound more completely than he bargained for?"

"Bondage is not necessarily the S/M of sadism and masochism. I subscribe to the definition of S/M as sensuality and mutuality. I have a printed contract. My bondage bottom signs it before the scene: 'From such-a-time to such-a-time, so-and-so is the property of so-and-so,' namely me, 'who has my uncoerced adult consent to do the following' and then we spell it all out: thick ropes, thin ropes, heavy chain, dental floss bondage of every single tooth in his head, hand and foot bondage, barbed wire around his chest and dick. Whatever is his fantasy. Whatever is our pleasure."

"Sounds like a prenuptial agreement," I say. "Very civilized."

"To my bondage-top mind, the bondage slave presents himself as a gift to be wrapped by the bondage master." He smiles a smile that makes me want to blow him. "To many men, just beginning bondage, to some intermediate rope-freaks, and even to heavy restraint addicts there comes a surprise."

"The best surprise is a thrill."

"The gift gets a gift."

"Silver threads? Golden needles? What?" I try not to show how much I appreciate any man who has his trip together not only physically, but also has scoped his fetish out analytically. A lot of guys can get at a man's body but lack the *head* to take over his mind.

And isn't that what guys stand around bars for until last call?

Just waiting, not for the Perfect Body to walk in, but the Perfect combination of Head and Body that can sweep them away, even for just a night, toward an unusual destiny.

Just to let go of your head and body.

Just to know a force outside you has taken over the responsibility of your body so totally that he restrains your brains.

Just a need to let go. Just a need to surrender control.

At least to glide into a space of trust for a while.

"Men have a need to give."

"Especially in a world with a shortage of takers, of guys who have a talent to take—in the best sense of the word."

He knots a perfect noose.

Signs and omens are everywhere.

"Bondage is not just sexual stimulation," he says. "The bondage top is father, teacher, lover, disciplinarian. He takes control in a world that seems out of control. The slave gives his very being. To be tied up is to be totally helpless."

A kind of sweet claustrophobia runs down my spine. Would a good gonzo writer allow himself to get tied up at this point for the sake of journalism?

"To be tied up is to be totally helpless, totally dependent. Lots of adult American males really ought to get themselves into this space: to physically and mentally surrender to somebody. By being a slave, a man finds out that there is a master. By giving up control, he finds a controller. By letting go, he finds ways of hanging on."

"There are holes in your logic," I say. "Maybe existential holes."

"Why?" He loops the rope into knots no sailor ever knew.

"Because I want there to be holes in your logic."

"Are you afraid I sound like I want to tie you up?"

"Yeah. You sound like you want to tie me up."

"There's not a body on earth that doesn't look better when tied into bondage sculpture."

"The strain on the muscles? The chest heaving deep for breath?" Am I leading him on?

"You don't like that?" He caresses the ropes.

"My head is afraid of it."

"What about your cock?" He smiles. He looks awful good.

"It's hard."

"You let your head do all your thinking?"

"I should maybe just follow my cock around?"

"Sometimes," he says, "maybe you have to trust not your head, but your cock."

"Maybe I'm just outside your fetish area. Maybe I'm like most guys who are afraid of the sexual activity that seems far out to them. Maybe a guy has to be a natural-born bondage freak."

"Any man can learn the sensuality of bondage. Just like guys learn the erotic sensuality of their earlobes, assholes, tits. A lot of sexual things, high sexual things, not just garden-variety blow-job sex, are the result of working at something to learn it, to acquire a taste for it."

"So," I say, "a guy who never thought much about bondage maybe ought to play out a scene to see how his taste might develop?"

"I look for that kind of guy. A man willing to learn something new. I like to work with, work on, seduce a man into enjoying something he never thought he'd like. Take Lawrence of Arabia getting tied down, whipped, and fucked. That had never happened to Lawrence before. The Arabs thought Lawrence would hate it. Lawrence thought Lawrence would hate it. Lawrence got a surprise. He liked it!"

"What about the American POWs in 'Nam? The Viet Cong used heavy and prolonged bondage on a lot of them. What do you think of that situation?"

"I think," he hesitates. "No. I know that out of all those tied up young fliers, sheer percentages mean that at least a few got off in their heads and their cocks on the bondage despite what their straight patriotic programming was."

"You think a lot of men need restraint, want bondage, and don't fully realize what it is they're looking for. You think bondage would directly relieve the tension of the lives they're living?"

He looks hard at me. "How do you spell real security?" he asks.

"B-o-n-d-a-g-e is the answer you want."

"Men need to know the limits. Especially in a totally permissive society. Bondage is a very physical means of limiting a man's activity. Some criminoid types are criminal for a main subconscious reason: deep down they really like, and need, to get handcuffed by a couple Big-Daddy cops who tell them they've gone too far and who toss them naked into a dark isolation cell in solitary."

"Madness takes its toll."

"Think about it," he says. "Think about those cops. Anybody who is a cop gets off on it. Cops like bondage. They study restraint techniques. They practice handcuffing each other. They get off on steel-mesh cages. Guys don't do jobs like that unless they're getting off on it at some level."

"I've read about military bondage in Navy SERE training."

"Then you'll like this. At the USMC brig at Camp Pendleton, the guards hog-tie the military prisoners, hands behind the back, wrists tied together and pulled down, then tied to the ankles pulled up behind the butt. Then they wrap the prisoner's head with white adhesive tape. Think about it: a young Marine, stripped to his skivvies and boots, with his head mummified completely except for his nostrils. He can't see. He can't yell. He can't move. He's left in an isolation box. What's he gonna do? Go crazy with claustrophobia, or, when he can't beat it, join it and get off on it? You think those MPs don't get off on doing that surgical-tape number? Hell, they don't do what they don't like. They just wrap their activity in God and Flag and anything goes. Overt sex may be very subliminal, but it's there just the same."

"Last summer," I say, "it wasn't so subliminal. Seven USMC officers were court-martialed for bringing Marine recruits into L.A. for sex acts and to make sex movies."

"Not much has changed since I was an MP."

"So what kind of guy do you prefer to tie up?"

"A decent body. A good head. A willingness to be sensual. An ability to trust. Mostly, I look for a sense of vulnerability."

"Vulnerability?"

"Vulnerability. That's what most bondage masters want, because the master is going to make the guy even more vulnerable. Bondage is not just a bedroom game. Bondage is an actualizing of fantasy. Bondage is living a lifestyle. It is living. It is the reality for the time the slave is in service. It is a symbol of man's real place in the whole universe."

"A friend of mine says bondage is unnatural," I say. "He says movement is the essence of life."

"A typical American attitude: movement for the sake of moving. Of course, he's right—if gross movements of arms and legs and running around is what he means. Jesus! Today's religion is jogging. What's everybody running to or from? A little more contemplative restraint, a little more bondage, and people might find out a bit more about themselves."

He wears full leather and sits like a man who knows his way around certain nighttime worlds.

"Your friend is right," he says, "if he defines life's essential movement as the flow of blood inside the body, as the run of electrical impulses through the nervous system. Bondage restrains the arms and the legs, slows down a guy's run-around attitude, so he can tune in to the more subtle aspects of his being."

"What is this?" I ask. "*Zen and the Art of Bondage Maintenance?*"

"Close to it. The Orientals are masters of bondage."

"I wouldn't know," I lie. "I've never been a rice queen."

"Our mutual friend said you spent part of last year in Japan."

"He spilled the egg rolls, huh?"

"Everything." He coils the rope around his big hand.

"Everything." I consider that a minute. "I spent a night at a Samurai House of Bondage outside Tokyo."

"Then you know."

"I just pinned on my Downed-American-Flier fantasy and let the Samurai bondage master do his trip for the assembled group." I'm gaining his interest by the minute.

"You liked the quality of the Japanese bondage?"

"I liked the exhibitionism of being a six-foot-one hundred-sixty-pound American male displayed immobile in a roomful of Asian men." I look at him. I try to read his face. "How's that," I ask, "for a true confession?"

"Did you cum?"

"What kind of question is that?" I get indignant fast when the answer is yes.

"A revealing one. The answer will tell me where you head is."

"Where my head was—for the appropriate occasion."

"Did you cum?" Insistence shines in his dark eyes.

"Yes," I surrender. "I came. Yeah. The bondage master ordered one of the other men, a very young well-muscled Yakuza type..."

"What," he interrupts, "is a Yakuza?"

"A Yakuza is a member of the Japanese Mafia. The guys have tattoos on both shoulders down past the biceps, down the sides of the torso, and around both thighs. Hot."

"Very hot."

"This Yakuza with the ritual tattoos held a vibrator against my fundoshi."

"Fundoshi?"

"The Japanese underwear, about six feet long, that wraps tight around your crotch like a jockstrap. The bondage master wanted the Yakuza to make me cum."

"You didn't want to?"

"The Japanese are very polite. The bondage master would have been insulted if I hadn't shot."

"Are you polite enough to allow me to restrain you completely, supposing I wanted to?"

"I came to Los Angeles to run around and see the sights and meet a lot of guys and go to the bars; thirty-six hours is a long time out of a week's visit."

"I'll bet you went to run around Tokyo, too. If you let me tie you up, you might slow down enough to figure out that a long intense scene with one guy is better than superficial nuptials with one hundred guys."

"Bondage scares some guys. Bondage has a lot of implications: trust, betrayal, gagging, panic. Implications have consequences. Some guys could get scared and freak out. Maybe I'm too claustrophobic to share your trip."

"I guarantee you'd feel good."

"What if the building catches fire? What if you have a heart attack?"

"What if the sky falls?" In the corner, a complete suspension harness hangs waiting.

"So I'm playing Devil's Advocate against bondage. I mean most guys don't understand it. Explain it if you can. I'm a quick study. I like to think I'm a sensualist. But frankly, if you tied me up—hysteria."

"Really?"

"Maybe."

"Hysteria is an honest bondage stage to pass through. When the body is restrained, the mind starts doing a number on itself. That's why druglessness is really a part of the sensitivity of the prolonged bondage trip. As you pass with full awareness through the bondage steps, you discover that the confining experience becomes an expanding experience. Since the bondage scene, immobile, gagged, and hooded, is essentially an external sense-deprivation trip, I find that not only bondage itself, but the longer bondage trip especially, appeals to guys who are more sensitive and aware of themselves. When you are tied three to four hours in one position, unable to hear, see, speak, or touch, and are touched only to be manipulated into a new position, your mind floats back into an almost womb-remembered state."

"I've read John Lilly's *Center of the Cyclone* about sensory-deprivation tanks and Ernest Becker's *Denial of Death,* which is about death—which is what my doctor told me to avoid at all costs."

"Maybe you read too much."

"They're both good books. They say almost exactly what you say. They say about life in general what you say about bondage in particular."

"No shit," he says.

"There's a life-lesson to unravel here in bondage."

"I'll tell you a life lesson. A sperm shot down a narrow penis canal gets caught in an ovum bound to the wall of a womb. Life starts in bondage. We're locked down in bondage by the gravity of this planet. We're buried in bondage."

"If you saw the movie *Coma*," he continues, "you saw real Medical Bondage. In Washington, D.C., some years back, an Army mathematician by the name of Stan Wilks spent seventy-two days in suspended animation. Doctors at George Washington University Hospital intentionally paralyzed him with his consent. They used curare, the drug Brazilian Indians use on blowgun darts. For seventy-two fucking days, Wilks was totally conscious, but he couldn't move an eye, blink, utter a single sound, move a muscle, or even breathe without a respirator."

"Doctors are very kinky," I say. "If we're going to play

'Can You Top This,' I know of this straight bodybuilder in San Francisco. His father's a cop. Ever since this kid—his name's Mike Dayton—was twelve or so, his father's been coaching his workouts: bodybuilding, tai chi. His dad, the cop, has been hanging him by the neck in the garage since he was a teenager. Mike's the only guy alive strong enough to break a pair of regulation police handcuffs. A couple summers ago, when he was about twenty-four, Mike was scheduled to be hanged by the neck at the Concord Pavilion. I was going to take the BART train, but Mike wasn't allowed to be hanged in public because all those Bay Area suburban parents feared their kids might try it."

"Bondage is as American as stocks in colonial Salem, and as contemporary as flogging teenage delinquents in Delaware. Bondage is necessary for a good whipping." He pulls out a recent news photo of some foreign cop convicted of taking bribes, stripped, and being flogged by another heavyweight cop in a courtyard. The bondage rack, to hold the man secure for the beating, shows frequent use.

In turn, I pull out my scrapbook and show him the following items.

- Police found a man bound to a tree in the woods early yesterday. He told the officers he had been tied for more than twelve hours. When police attempted to cut the chains, he refused their aid, saying that the men who had bound him were coming back, but had been scared off by the arrival of the squad cars.
- On Hampstead Heath, outside London, men are frequently found tied to trees or staked out. One man, found crucified by police after midnight, refused their aid and they left him, since they knew the nature of the Heath after dark.

• In San Francisco, a man was found dead, hog-tied on Diamond Heights. The noose around his neck had been pulled tight by the rope around his ankles, The *Chronicle* entitled the article: "A Fondness for Knots was the Death of Him."

"Everybody," he says, "is into our act. Nancy Grossman gets grants from the National Endowment for the Arts for her leather-bondage sculpture. She deserves it. Hot stuff. I've seen her sculpture used at West Hollywood orgies."

"The San Francisco Ballet," I say, "took bondage out of its closet. In its premier of *Trilogy*, four male dancers raised a very muscular Gardner Carlson into total bondage suspension. In the finale, Carlson, nearly naked, was discovered slung high in a harness over stage center. The four men, manipulating the ropes tied to his wrist and ankles, jerked him up, down, around, every which way. The audience loved it.

"A reviewer called 'the mood tense and terrifying: man as marionette or a wild prisoner/animal. Caught in this cat's cradle. Carlson is jerked spread-eagle with excruciating force. Then he's spun around upside down.' And on goes the critical bullshit," I say.

"Rona Barrett said on Mike or Merv or one of those clone-host talk shows that the reason 'Roots' was so popular was that 'America has a love affair with bondage,' " he says.

"The Theater Workers of San Francisco presented Brecht's translation of Marlowe's *Edward II* with an ad of a naked blond man suspended upside down with chains. I liked that."

"Everybody," he says, "needs such a large bush to beat around. Everybody tries to intellectualize everything. Why can't people just admit that bondage looks good and feels good?"

"Tennessee Williams in *Night of the Iguana* has two hot

Mexican boys tie the hero into a hammock. He pushes them away but their arms are strong and dark. They bind him tight with rope drawn through the weave of the hammock. He's screaming that 'People just want to see a man in a tied-up situation.'

"The boys wrap another twenty feet of rope around the man lurching in a horizontal stretch between two heavy wooden posts. They stand back and share a cigarette. They stare at their handiwork exhausting himself into a sweat in the hot tropical night. They laugh, turn, and leave him. 'Everybody,' he repeats until his voice is almost gone, 'wants to see a man in a tied up situation.' "

"Bondage is everywhere. The Nick Nolte movie *Who'll Stop the Rain?* has guys handcuffed to toilets and water heaters and trucks. There used to be, maybe still is, although I haven't seen it for a while, a Canadian rag called *The Justice Weekly*."

"What's best these days," I say, "is the *Rigid Bondage Roster*." It has ads like:

- Experienced white male Master, 30s, 6', into deep S/M trip; digs strict discipline, whips, heavy extended bondage, immobilization in leather, rubber, steel, boots, hoods, cages; seeks contacts with male slaves who dig being tied up all night.
- White male, 40, enjoys lengthy bondage, leather, ropes, chains. Wants slave. No sex. No money. Only bondage: to be bound and to bind you.
- Sam. S. Experienced in heavy bondage, seeks groovy studs to submit to extended periods of bondage and sex. I am fully equipped in rope, leather, steel, and genitoys to keep it all nicely together. There is nothing more frightening than ignorance in action.

"Put your ass where your mouth is," he says. "You read about bondage. You jerk off in movies to bondage. You talk about bondage. You study bondage. You write about bondage. You're a bondage top. Maybe. But you'll be a better bondage top if you, for one good time, were a total bondage bottom."

"You know what you're doing," I say. "Our mutual friend respects you."

"To quote your quote," he says, " 'There is nothing more frightening than ignorance in action.' "

"You sure as hell ain't ignorant."

"So what do you say?"

I look around his apartment. Everything is in perfect readiness. I might say yes. I might say, "Let's call up one of your regular bottoms and both tie him up." But then again if I only go around once in life...

"So what do you say?"

"I say: You're a big six feet and two hundred pounds. I say: I'm easily seduced by a man who can talk his way into my head. I say: I like a man who tries to top a top. I say: I think we both have a sense of humor about this. I say: the essence of homomutuality is that we're never into anything too far that we can't turn back. I say: I notice you're unplugging my cassette recorder."

"You sure say a lot," he says.

"I say: this is the sexy part in the movies where the camera moves away from the couple and focuses on the waves crashing on the shore, on the trees blowing in the wind...."

"And," he says, "on the train rushing headlong into the dark tunnel."

ABOUT THE AUTHORS

SHANE ALLISON's stories have graced the pages of *Best Black Gay Erotica*, *Best Gay Erotica 2007* and *2008*, *Ultimate Gay Erotica 2006, 2007* and *2008*, and more than a dozen other anthologies. He is the editor of *Hot Cops* and *Backdraft: Fireman Erotica*.

BILL BRENT's sex-and-drugs memoir, "This Insane Allure," comprises one-seventh of *Entangled Lives: Memoirs of 7 Top Erotic Authors*; it would make a dandy graphic novel—any publishers interested? His nonfiction article, "Martin Luther Goes Bowling," appears in *Everything You Know about God Is Wrong*. He is also author of *The Ultimate Guide to Anal Sex for Men*. "Other People's Women" appears in *More Five-Minute Erotica*, and "Yummy" appears in *Leathermen*, edited by Simon Sheppard. He has completed one novel, about a drug-dealing whoreboy who runs away from his clients and girlfriend to join the circus. Follow Bill's antics at LitBoy.com.

JACK FRITSCHER, the founding San Francisco editor-in-chief of *Drummer* magazine and its most frequent contributor (1975-1999), is the pioneer author of a hundred BDSM stories and articles, the photographer of a thousand published S/M photographs, and the screenwriter-director of two hundred BDSM videos. Author of the books *Gay San Francisco* and *Some Dance to Remember: A Memoir-Novel of San Francisco*, he is the surviving bicoastal lover and biographer of photographer Robert Mapplethorpe, legendary for his fetish, face, and flower photographs. Visit www.jackfritscher.com.

SHANNA GERMAIN is a poet by nature, a short-story writer by the skin of her teeth, and a novelist in training. Her award-winning writing has appeared in places like Salon, *Absinthe Literary Review*, *Best American Erotica 2007*, *Best Gay Romance 2008*, *Best Lesbian Erotica 2008*, *The Mammoth Book of Best New Erotica*, *Rubber Sex*, and *Bedding Down*. You can read more about her at www.shannagermain.com.

DOUG HARRISON's erotic ruminations, which complement his opera fairydom and offset his PhD in optical engineering, appear in zines and more than a dozen anthologies. His memoir, *In Pursuit of Ecstasy*, appears in *The Shadow Sacrament: a journal of sex and spirituality*. Doug was active in San Francisco's leather scene and the Modern Primitives movement. He appears in videos, photo shoots, and an AIDS Emergency Fund's Bare Chest Calendar, and is a member of the Chicago Hellfire Club. He now lives in warm Hawaii, where his most difficult sartorial decision is which color jock or thong to wear. Find him at pumadoug@hawaii.rr.com.

WILLIAM HOLDEN is LGBT studies librarian at Emory University in Atlanta. He has served as fiction editor for *RFD* magazine, has completed five bibliographies for the American Library Association's GLBT Roundtable and has written more than twenty works of gay short fiction.

DAVID HOLLY's stories have been printed in gay erotic magazines including *Guys, Firsthand, Manscape,* and *Hot Shots*, and in anthologies from Alyson Books and Cleis Press.

JEFF MANN's books include two collections of poetry, *Bones Washed with Wine* and *On the Tongue*; a book of personal essays, *Edge*; a novella, "Devoured," included in *Masters of Midnight*; a collection of poetry and memoir, *Loving Mountains, Loving Men*; and a volume of short fiction, *A History of Barbed Wire*, winner of a Lambda Literary Award. He is an associate professor of creative writing at Virginia Tech in Blacksburg, Virginia.

SEAN MERIWETHER enjoys living up to his moniker as the "Naughty Harry Potter." He has been working his own brand of magic, crafting immersive fiction and erotica that transports boys and girls into the tumescent landscape of his wicked imaginings. He has published more than forty short stories in venues including *Best of Best Gay Erotica 2, Best Gay Love Stories 2006,* and Lodestar Quarterly. He is completing work on his collection, *The Silent Hustler*.

LEN RICHMOND created one of England's most successful sitcoms, "Agony," about the tribulations of a pot-smoking advice columnist, which won the AGLA Media Award for the "responsible portrayal of its gay and lesbian characters." He recently wrote and directed the independent feature film *A*

Dirty Little Business. Set in the sex-toy biz, it stars Michael York, Andy Bell, and Beverly D'Angelo. He is coeditor of *The Gay Liberation Book* and author of the erotic novel *Naked in Paradise* (Sybaritic Press), from which "Straight As a Question Mark" is excerpted.

SIMON SHEPPARD is the editor of *Homosex: Sixty Years of Gay Erotica* and the forthcoming *Leathermen*, and the author of *In Deep: Erotic Stories, Kinkorama: Dispatches from the Front Lines of Perversion, Sex Parties 101,* and *Hotter Than Hell and Other Stories,* winner of the Erotic Author Association's Award for Best Single-Author Collection. His work also appears in more than two hundred and fifty anthologies, including many editions of *The Best American Erotica* and *Best Gay Erotica.* He writes the syndicated column "Sex Talk" and the online serial "The Dirty Boys Club," owns a well-used set of restraints, and hangs out at www.simonsheppard.com.

J. M. SNYDER writes gay erotic/romantic fiction and has self-published several books in the genre, though more recent books have been e-published through Aspen Mountain, Amber Quill, and Torquere Presses. More information at www. jmsnyder.net.

JAY STARRE resides on English Bay in Vancouver, Canada, and writes erotic fiction stories for gay men's magazines including *Men* and *Torso.* Jay has also written gay fiction for more than forty-five anthologies, including *Best Gay Romance 2008, Travelrotica, Manhandled,* and *Bear Lust.*

ETHAN THOMAS is the penname of two writers living in Alberta, Canada. Like their chocolate, they prefer their writing dark, and believe the horror and erotic genres can be perfectly combined. Partnered for two years but having lived together for only one, they spend their spare time fighting lost causes on the Internet and haunting local curio shops. They are the proud owners of three pets, one of which they occasionally let drive the car. Together they form the editing team of Thaneros, an online magazine dedicated to dark erotica.

LARRY TOWNSEND is best known as author of the *The Leatherman's Handbook*, first published in 1972 by Olympia Press, and *Leatherman's Handbook II*, released ten years later by Carlyle Communications, both still in print. He has written more than forty other books and established his own small press in the early seventies, L. T. Publications, publishing 74 large format books by himself and others. He continues to write a monthly advice column for *Honcho* magazine. Larry was a well-known activist in the gay movement during the seventies and early eighties, as president of H.E.L.P., Inc. and as founding president of The Hollywood Hills Democratic Club, the first gay-oriented club in Los Angeles County. *TimeMasters*, a new science fiction novel, was published in 2008 (Booksurge), with a sequel in the works. His partner of 44 years, Fred, passed away last year.

TRUDEVIANT's stories have appeared in *BUTT, Tough Guys, Bad Boys, Porn, Saints and Sinners, Sex Buddies, Best Bisexual Erotica, Love Under Foot, The Wildest Ones,* and *Black Sheets.*

ALANA NOËL VOTH is a single mom who lives in Oregon with her son, three cats, and several freshwater fish. Her stories have appeared in *Best Gay Erotica 2004, 2007,* and *2008, Where the Boys Are: Urban Gay Erotica, The Mammoth Book of Best New Erotica Volume 7, I Is for Indecent, Best Amer-*

ican Erotica 2005, Best Women's Erotica 2004, Best Bisexual Women's Erotica, Best Lesbian Love Stories, Cleansheets, *Desdmona, Oysters and Chocolate*, Blithe House Quarterly, *The Big Stupid Review, Literary Mama*, and *Eclectica Magazine*. Hit her blog at http://marsmarsvenus.blogspot.com.

ANDREW WARBURTON is a PhD student specializing in literary theory. Until recently he worked as a copywriter, research assistant, and reporter in London, but has moved to the United States to continue his studies. His short stories have appeared in *Hustlers: Erotic Stories of Sex for Hire* and *Boys in Heat*, while his poetry has been published in the queer literary journal *Chroma*.

ABOUT THE
EDITOR

RICHARD LABONTÉ reads and reviews many books, reads and edits many, many short stories and essays for assorted anthologies, and lives with his husband Asa on Bowen Island, British Columbia. Contact him at tattyhill@gmail.com.